Already a published author, Mary has been writing from a very young age. Having had poetry as well as fiction published, she has also written song lyrics. Married to Declan, Mary likes to spend quality time walking with their golden shepherd, Jaz. Living in the Claddagh in Galway City, she appreciates and is inspired by the beauty of Galway Bay.

I would like to dedicate this book to my sister, Evelyn. Taken too soon but thought of everyday. This one's for you, Ev x.

Mary Finnerty-Morris

VALERIE

AUSTIN MACAULEY PUBLISHERS™
LONDON • CAMBRIDGE • NEW YORK • SHARJAH

Copyright © Mary Finnerty-Morris 2023

The right of Mary Finnerty-Morris to be identified as the author of this work has been asserted by the author in accordance with sections 77 and 78 of the Copyright, Designs and Patents Act 1988.

All rights reserved. No part of this publication may be reproduced, stored in a retrieval system, or transmitted in any form or by any means, electronic, mechanical, photocopying, recording, or otherwise, without the prior permission of the publishers.

Any person who commits any unauthorised act in relation to this publication may be liable to criminal prosecution and civil claims for damages.

A CIP catalogue record for this title is available from the British Library.

ISBN 9781398432109 (Paperback)
ISBN 9781398432116 (Hardback)
ISBN 9781398432123 (ePub e-book)

www.austinmacauley.com

First Published 2023
Austin Macauley Publishers Ltd®
1 Canada Square
Canary Wharf
London
E14 5AA

I would like to acknowledge a good friend of ours, Paul Curran who rescued me when I thought I had lost my manuscript through a virus on my laptop. Thanks, Paul.

Chapter 1

"Hi, Valerie…it's June." Her hand was shaking as she held the phone.

Hoping that her mother would be glad to hear from her.

What if she wasn't, she'd thought what if?

The voice on the other end of the phone had put an end to her wondering.

"I'm sorry dear…you must have the wrong number…there's no Valerie here I'm afraid."

June thanked the lady for her time and hung up. Matilda was cleaning the tables in Tilly's as she left the phone down. "Everything ok, June?"

She must have looked dazed she'd felt dazed, it had taken her all of this time not to mention all of her strength to dial that number and to no avail!

"Oh…I'm fine Matilda…just fine…" She hurriedly made her way to the door she needed air, she felt like she hadn't taken a breath since she'd dialled that number she was filling up, this had been such a shock to her.

Valerie must have moved on, deep in thought walking back to the post office she decided she must pull herself together and move on too, if Valerie had wanted her to contact her surely she would have left a forwarding address or number or something!

Aidan her manager, seemed a decent enough sort unlike Mr Oakley the new owner of the post office. Mac was so easy going, wouldn't have to run to Tilly's to make a phone call with Mac around, not that she ever took advantage.

But with Mr Oakley breathing down her neck one would not take any such liberties. Whatever about her sad life she was only passing the time there, but Aidan a young man with everything going for him, why he put up with the abuse she could never understand.

"He's ok really…just a bit of a perfectionist I guess…" Aidan would take all the criticising he'd give him and he'd given him plenty.

Mr Oakley had taken over a string of shops over the years apparently, *a shrewd businessman,* June thought, hadn't a bit of nature in him. It wasn't the nice friendly post office anymore with the locals coming in, more for a chat than a purchase. June recalled Mrs Beatty coming in back in the day when Clodagh was around, or even when Mac had the business it was just the same by the time she'd passed on all the gossip she'd have forgotten what she'd come in for in the first place. Nancy didn't come with the daffodils now either, June felt the old customers were of no interest to Mr Oakley he'd brush past them in the food aisle and nearly take them with him sometimes he'd be in such a hurry.

The customers had felt it too, often June would chat to them just to annoy him. Never one to criticise but he did annoy her, it didn't take much to be friendly after all, they were keeping his little business going. *He was a strange character,* she'd thought. Greta had come in with her lovely fresh eggs only to be told to take them to the market to sell them, he could be hurtful at times.

Having come straight from the back garden after collecting the eggs Greta was wearing wellies and an old overcoat, he'd looked at her as if he was disgusted.

June had been thinking of a change for a while now. She wasn't happily working there anymore she remembered a time when she'd look forward to going into work. Didn't even feel like work then, she'd be kept on top of all that was going on with the local gossips she'd loved the chats she'd have with them.

If anything was keeping her in that job, it was the few who still came in to shop there and there were only the few now.

She'd felt a sort of loyalty towards them and didn't want to let them down.

In time she would find something else she was sure of it, she would have to put up with the misery for a while longer.

Aidan was a lovely young lad, had trained in business management in college. There weren't many opportunities around these parts so he was happy to take on the job, June got on well with him she'd thought he'd thought of her as a sort of a mother figure. He'd come in after being out at the weekend with all his tales of woe, she had become very fond of him and she loved hearing his stories.

She often thought had she married and had children of her own they would probably be around that age now, well maybe not quite but near enough, she wondered if they would have come to her with their stories of the night before. She hoped they might. She would have loved to have had children.

She hoped Aidan would someday take her advice and find a job where his qualifications would be appreciated, they certainly weren't now. He'd smile and say he was putting it all down to experience.

She thought of Valerie and her phone call earlier that week. She wondered if she would ever see her again and she wondered why she even cared.

Valerie obviously didn't!

She had pondered for a long time before she'd decided to make that call, maybe too long. She took the slip of paper out of her pocket now almost worn to a thread it being folded for so long, she thought of the day her mother gave it to her. A long time ago now, looking closely she wondered if the crease in the paper had made the zero look like an eight. What if it had! What if she had dialled the wrong number! Walking by Tilly's on the way home she wanted to go in to try ringing the number again, this time putting a zero where she'd thought there was an eight, but she couldn't bear to think that she would be disappointed again.

Greta was waiting at the bus stop as June walked by.

"Going into the city?" June wished she'd had the energy to be off out into town herself but she couldn't wait to get her feet off the ground.

"No, lovey…I'm going in to meet an old friend…have a cup of tea and an old chat…you know…mind you if I was able… I would be taking my business into town these days rather than the post office."

"…it's just so handy there though…wouldn't have the energy to be traipsing around the city…but that fella…Oakley…wouldn't you love to tell him to cheer up…the Lord save us and bless us but he's miserable…"

June had to laugh at her, true as it was.

"…enjoy!" She waved goodbye and left her rooting in her purse for change.

It was hard to put an age on Greta, June thought to herself but she'd remembered her saying she'd gone to school with Valerie. She would have to be near enough sixty she'd thought, though she looked older somehow.

Greta looked down the road after June as the bus approached, she had wanted to tell her she was going into town to meet her mother as she had done at least once a month since Valerie had left. They'd always kept in touch if not in person by post, although thinking back to that day that she'd put her foot into it with June in talking about her grandmother and how she was so good to take a young baby on at her age; she'd sworn she would never mention Valerie again.

Valerie would always want the latest news on June, Greta often thought it was the main reason she'd kept in touch but she'd never wanted June's grandmother or June to know. Whatever Greta thought of the situation, Valerie was her lifelong friend and she'd trusted her and wasn't going to betray her trust and that was that.

Passing old Walter's house as June still called it she'd felt a pang of loneliness, now occupied by a young couple with three young children. She hadn't seen much of the mam and dad but the children would often wave out of the window as she passed by, there were two girls and a boy.

Although June hadn't really befriended them in any way, she always got the feeling that the dad was a bit strange, a bit cagey. She remembered Matt used to say she was a people watcher, if they'd be out anywhere, she'd often comment on a couple in passing maybe in the way they would look at each other or not look at each other.

"They're fighting," she would say and Matt would laugh. Dear Matt!

A lifetime ago now, she wondered about his mother she would maybe write her a letter see how his dad was. She would put a return address on it so that she could write back, last time she had received a letter from Matt's mother was through Walter, dear old Walter!

Writing her return address on the back of the envelope she had posted the letter to Matt's mother only to have it returned within a couple of weeks, within a larger envelope with another letter inside as well.

"I'm returning this letter with regret in having to tell you that Mrs Deegan is no longer living here." The letter went on to say that the new tenant had been in the house for a few months now and had no details of the people who lived there before him and apologised.

June thought it was so kind of him to reply he needn't have bothered and she wondered what had brought about such a change, what had happened to Matt's mother! Had the dad passed away and she'd moved? Surely not, she would have contacted her, she'd left her the number of the post office in case she ever needed her. She would have to find out, but how?

Aidan was in bright and early the next morning, and well and truly settled into work by the time June arrived. Greeting her with a smile.

"Morning." She knew by his face that he'd had Mr Oakley on his back already.

"Hi Aidan...you were in early I'd say?" June made her way to her desk quite swiftly as Mr Oakley came out of nowhere looking at his watch. She wasn't late she'd thought to herself, not even a good morning just a grunt to make her aware of his presence, he could be so rude.

Aidan winked at her and it was head down after that, takings were down at month's end and Mr Oakley was even more irate than usual.

June remembering her school days, if she'd got up early at the weekend when there was no school her pop would say, "Good morning…did you wet the bed?" They would laugh pop was so kind, had a lovely way about him. In looking at Mr Oakley he would have been about the same age as her pop was then, but what a different temperament.

What was it that had this man so angry with the world?

Matt's mother came to mind as she took her key out of her bag and saw the letter, it had rained all morning so she thought she would put her key in her coat pocket to save her rooting for it in the rain when she got home. She remembered the lady in the shop where the bus had stopped that day that she went to visit Matt's mother, she seemed to know the family.

She would take the bus on Saturday and go to see if she could find out where they'd moved to. There was absolutely no reason in the world for her to be concerned about them, she'd only met the woman a couple of times and had never actually met Matt's dad, but she cared. Maybe it was out of loyalty to Matt, she wasn't sure but she had thought of them on and off and was now genuinely concerned that they no longer lived there. The shop was busy as she entered so she looked at some magazines while waiting for a chance to talk to the woman behind the counter. She was the same woman, as June got off the bus the thought had entered her head.

"What if that same woman wasn't in the shop!"

It was a chance to take in going all that way but there was no other way, it was a long shot. She was relieved to see the same woman there.

"Oh! deary me...sure poor Ellen passed away...oh it's near on a year now dear...sure it was so sad." She'd stuck June to the floor.

"...the old lad sure he was taken into a nursing home...no one to look after him..." June didn't know what to say.

"...here sit down dear...sit down..." As if she'd seen the shock in her face, the woman took June by the arm and led her behind the counter to her chair.

"...let me lock the door...sure t'is time for the lunch anyway...you know they'd come in here last minute sometimes...wouldn't think you had a mouth on you at all yourself...now...can I get you some tea..." She was off and disappeared before June had a chance to answer. They talked for the best part of an hour and June thanked her for her time and for the tea, it was much appreciated she'd said.

"...not at all lovey...it was a bit of a shock for you. I could see it in your face a girl...God bless you now and take care..." The woman walked her to the door and took the 'Closed' sign down.

The next bus wouldn't be leaving for an hour so June walked about for a while, it was a lovely little village typical of the countryside. A local shop a pub and a chapel with a graveyard to the rear. June wondered if maybe Matt's mother would have been buried there, she would take a stroll around. It wasn't a big graveyard but then it was a very small village, it was well kept with most graves having fresh flowers on them. She would visit nan's and pop's grave when she got back, bring fresh flowers.

"Matt Deegan."

Beloved son of Ellen and Matthew…

Rest in Peace.

June felt a cold chill come over her as she continued to read beneath Matt's name.

"Ellen Deegan."

Beloved wife and mother.

Rest in Peace.

Her legs felt like jelly as she lowered herself to sit on the curb of the grave. He should be enjoying his young life, having his dreams come true laughing and living. He should be with her, there was an eerie stillness about the place. She touched the clay—took a piece of it in her hand as if to feel something, touch something!

Getting to her feet she ran until she reached the gate of the graveyard and stopped to look back, finally she'd had closure maybe now in time her heart might heal.

She thought about the woman in the shop she hadn't even asked her, her name nor had she asked June hers. She'd told her how Ellen, Matt's mother had never been the same since Matt had been killed, she was lost she'd said.

Seems grief had taken its toll and folk had said she'd died of a broken heart. Found at the end of the stairs thought to have been tending to the dad after the night, the front door left open for fresh air. June remembered her saying how she used to do that when she'd visited her last time.

The nurse had found her but it was too late she had gone, had it been in years gone by the woman in the shop had said there would have been some suspicion alright.

"…she'd put up with that fella for years…walloping her in the droves of drink…many a time she'd come into the shop with a scarf over her mouth where he'd given her a clout…wouldn't be me…by God I'd swing for him," the lady in the shop had said.

"Aw…stop it was awful…and you can't interfere then…sure you'd be the worst in the world…poor Matt…that poor lad was driven away…driven away he was…"

Such a sad existence nobody deserved that June thought as the bus pulled up, she hadn't felt the journey back lost in her thoughts.

A glorious Sunday morning June hadn't been to mass for a while, she would go today and go by the shop and pick up some flowers for the grave.

It was peaceful there she thought about her nan and pop and the lovely relationship they'd had in life, she hoped they were together now in death and she wondered if death was the end?

Mrs Kelly was coming up the pathway pushing Mrs Beatty in the wheelchair huffing and puffing she was breathless as she approached.

"Isn't it great…the new ramp at the church…we can go to mass now without waiting for someone out of the kindness of their heart to lift the chair up the steps…it's great."

Her cheeks were rosy June wasn't sure if it was the fresh air or her blood pressure.

"Hello Mrs Kelly…and how are you Mrs Beatty?" June shook her hand as she put it out to her from under a blanket.

"I'm good now thanks June…I feel the cold sitting in this thing so I bring the blanket…"

It had been such a change for her to be depending on people to take her out now, not able to push it herself with her hands full of arthritis.

"Mrs Kelly is very good…indeed in everybody is very good to me…sure I'm lucky to be in it at all…walking out in front of the milk truck like that…what was I thinking…if I had my time over again…" June assured her that she need never be stuck and how lucky she was to have a friend like Mrs Kelly.

The weekend had gone so fast, June had hardly begun to relax what with the shock of hearing about Matt's mother and the reality of seeing Matt's name on a headstone. She had been totally unprepared.

She felt exhausted and yawned all through the day at work. She wondered about Clodagh she hadn't heard from her in a long time and because she moved around so much in her job now, she had to wait to hear from her to reply. She was thinking how unselfish she was to give up her time, her life really to go out to a country she knew nothing about to help the less fortunate.

She remembered the stories she had told her when she had come to stay with her the time she was struck down with malaria. Would make you think she thought to herself, any of us could have been born into it into the poverty, the sickness depravity, wars, and corruption. She wondered if she could ever up and leave like that do something good with her life, face and endure the danger and pain. Clodagh had expressed her sheer will and determination even at her weakest, she was hardly ready to go back there when she did but her courage had made her strong enough.

Fr Mulcahy was coming down the aisle of the chapel as June went in to light a candle on her way home, she couldn't get Matt's mother out of her mind so she said she'd light a candle for her, carrying his vestments after celebrating mass he was joyous as ever.

"Aw...t'is yourself that's in it, June...how's things with you? Working away?"

They'd chatted for a few minutes about this and that, Fr Mulcahy folding his vestments as they talked.

"Do you know, June, but I'm sweating bullets...it's like a sauna up on the alter wearing the vestments..." He wiped his face on his sleeve.

"Why the different colours, Father? The vestments I mean...sometimes you're wearing green...sometimes purple..." June knew she must have learned this stuff in school but she couldn't remember.

"You see, June...every different colour symbolises a different celebration or feast day or even a season...this green one now for instance symbolises hope and life...we wear green for masses in 'Ordinary Time'...or sometimes for a funeral. to symbolise life after death..."

"...it's not like I get up and look in my wardrobe and decide...I think I'll wear the red one today...or maybe the white one..." They both had a laugh and he was off.

It must be great to belong to something June thought to know that what you're doing is what you want to do, she would have to do some serious thinking about her position in life. She was merely existing she needed to find a purpose, at times she felt adrift.

She'd hoped that by finding her mother things might change, she might have someone. Maybe she had dialled the wrong number that day, maybe her mother was still waiting for her call.

"Have you seen, June…how is she doing?" Greta would be quizzed as usual by Valerie as she hugged her friend at the bus stop.

Valerie was greying at the temples now beginning to show her age a very attractive girl in her day.

Chapter 2

Greta always wished she'd had her figure. Only had to look at a bun and she would put on a few pounds but Valerie, she could eat till the cows come home with no ill effect.

"See her in the shop most days…haven't really been talking to her much…not since she passed me at the bus stop last time I came into town…" Greta wished things were different didn't seem right having a daughter and not be with her.

She knew in her heart that Valerie would love to get to know June, very much like herself they would get on like a house on fire Greta thought but it wasn't her place to interfere. She remembered when June's grandfather died and she'd gone to meet Valerie to tell her the news, there had been no show of emotion she'd had a fallen out with her herself then and told her to try to mend her fences with June's grandmother. Time moved on and there was no mending of fences, then it was too late the moment had passed. *Life is too short,* Greta thought to herself.

Valerie had contacted Greta a long time after that to enquire about how things were, Greta having had words with her on their last meeting hadn't contacted her before that.

Again too little too late June's grandmother (Valerie's mother) had too passed on.

It was then she'd told Greta that she would write to June and see if she would meet up with her. A meeting that would prove to be fruitless.

No word from her daughter no phone call.

June had coughed all night long she didn't know where she had picked up such a cold. There hadn't been anyone into the post office with a cold she didn't think, she would have noticed perhaps she'd picked up something on the bus on the way to see about Matt's mother. It was a miserable one anyway *wherever it had come from* she'd thought. Would she dare take the day off?

She did feel exhausted and really didn't want to go spreading her germs to someone else.

Not one to take time off work usually surely Mr Oakley would understand, it was early morning she'd seen every hour on the clock so she had decided to get up altogether. She would go and slip a note in the door of the post office and hope that Aidan would pick it up before Mr Oakley would get in. After a few hours of rest and a dose from the chemist she was feeling much better. Arriving at work the following day, not expecting sympathy from her employer she wasn't surprised that he barely acknowledged her presence. Glasses halfway down his nose he walked past her with his nose in the air. Aidan was nowhere to be seen June took up her place at the counter and was busy catching up from the day before when Aidan came in the door.

"Hey…you feeling better…missed you yesterday…"

He looked around as if to see if the coast was clear and with a smirk on his face he continued "…did you get a telling off? ... he wasn't impressed with your absence yesterday...sure the place would fall down without you..."

She wouldn't know if he was being funny or sarcastic or maybe a bit of both but at least he'd acknowledged her presence.

Greta came in to collect her pension. "Call by on your way home and I'll give you some fresh eggs..." June thought it was so nice of her.

Only in the door and she had the kettle on the boil. June was so glad to be out of the post office her mouth was drying up with the lack of conversation.

Greta had a laugh when she told her about the goings on in there.

"Why don't you get another job June...you'd be better off out of there...it 'isn't good for a person to be around people like that...sure you'd be depressed...it's bad for you now...I'm telling you..." June thought she was probably right she would have to do something about it.

"Maybe I'll take up baking...what do you think Greta...you can supply the fresh eggs and I'll do the rest..." June smiled as she buttered the fresh scone only out of the oven by the smell around the place.

This was so nice she'd become very close to Greta of late, she'd often thought of asking her about her mother she'd been in school with her she'd told her before. She would never have the nerve to ask her about her though, and sure that had been years ago anyway she probably wouldn't remember much.

Greta was thinking to herself if only Valerie could enjoy the company of her daughter as much as she had in these past few months. It had been her boss Mr Oakley that had brought them closer Greta remembered, *a strange sort of a man but something good had come of it*, she'd thought to herself. It was the first day she had brought her eggs to the post office since he'd taken over.

He'd more or less told her where to go with her eggs, June had followed her down the road to apologise for his rudeness and had said she would call after work for a chat. Since then she'd called by at least once in the week there wouldn't always be eggs to give her but there would always be a bit of home baking going. The hens had slowed down they weren't laying as much as they used to. Greta wasn't sure why *maybe they were stressed* she'd thought. The new neighbours now living in old Walter's house had cats, now Mrs Sheridan had a little cat Cheeky but she'd kept him in the house most of the time. He was never let to roam not like these ones, she'd hunted them off her wall a hundred times so maybe the poor hens were a bit stressed or maybe they were just getting old.

She loved to see June coming often she would see her walk by and be disappointed that she'd passed by without calling in but she knew she must be busy and she would be sure that she would call another day, and she always did.

June had many of her mother's traits her kind and thoughtful ways her concern for others and she had her looks too. Now a young woman Greta wondered why she choose to stay in these parts there was nothing around here for the likes of her. No opportunities to speak of but she seemed content to stay.

"…I must be off Greta…thank you for the lovely scones and the lovely fresh eggs…I should be buying them from you…are you making anything on them at all now?"

"...aw sure a girl...you wouldn't be making a living on them...the old hens are gone into retirement I think..." They both laughed and parted.

Closing the gate behind her, June waved back to Greta who had walked out behind her pulling at the weeds in the garden as she went.

"...that old chicken weed it has everything ruined..."

June had a thought and turned back.

"...let me know next time you're taking the bus into town and I'll go with you...could do with a few new bits...my wardrobe is looking a bit dated..." She waved and was off.

Greta could feel her face going red. Luckily, she was too far gone to notice.

She would be taking the bus on Friday afternoon but she was meeting Valerie.

"Aw, June...just the girl..." Millie was limping as she approached.

"You ok Millie...what's happened to your leg...?" She leaned against the wall as if using it as a crutch.

"...stop. I'm crippled...it's my hip...have to have surgery..." Milly went on to say that she wouldn't be returning to the 'Old Forge' after her surgery.

There would be a long recovery time and frankly she'd had enough. A bookkeeper for years there June remembered when Matt had come to town first, he covered for Millie in The Forge while she was out sick.

"...sure who am I working for...not a chick nor child to leave all my millions to." They both laughed.

"...was wondering if maybe you'd be interested in the job...you'd be well able for it...after all your years in the post office...and they say your new boss isn't the easiest to get along with…what do you think? …be a few weeks anyway yet sure give it a bit of thought."

June thanked her for thinking of her and assured her she would think about it for sure. The thought of walking away from the misery of working in the post office was indeed very pleasing to her but was she going from the frying pan into the fire!

She remembered Matt saying he was bored to tears the time he'd worked at the Forge when Milly was ill, seemed like a lifetime ago now.

Then there were her old customers that she felt depended on her, no she would bide her time as pop used to say, "The devil you know is better than the devil you don't know."

She was kinda getting used to Mr Oakley's moods now, she grew accustomed to his ways and sometimes rudeness, she would talk to Milly later.

Something would come up when the time was right; she was sure of it.

As usual Valerie was eager to hear any news regarding June as they sat in the window of the coffee shop on the corner. Greta told her how she had called in and she'd given her some fresh eggs and how they'd chatted and how she'd had to take a different route so as not to walk into her at the bus stop.

"I do wish you would come to visit her…you know…just for a chat."

Valerie assured her there was nothing she would rather do but as she had told her before June had her number if she wanted to get in touch and it would have to be her decision.

Valerie could get the smell of body odour across the table, Greta hadn't washed in a while she'd thought although she did look smart but the clean clothes had been put on over the dirt she'd thought. She wanted to say it to her as she had wanted so many times but it was so hard. Her hair too neglected pinned up at the side putting years on her. She was a nice-looking woman the odd time she did make an effort she would turn a head or two. Valerie wasn't sure what had happened along the way but when they were growing up Greta was as glamorous as the next. She always remembered her nails long and painted. Now you could grow potatoes underneath them there was so much muck, there was no need for that she'd thought there was no shortage of water as far as she was aware. She'd spoken to her a few times on the issue thinking as a friend she should. People would stare sometimes getting the whiff as they passed but each time she'd brought it up they'd fallen out, only to have Greta come back to her again full of apologies and promises to look after herself.

Milly fully understood that June had loyalty towards her customers and admired her for it, the position would be advertised and should she change her mind in the meantime she would put in a good word for her. June wished her well with her surgery and a speedy recovery and they would chat again soon.

Aidan had been to a party at the weekend and lost his wages, Mr Oakley offered him a few days in advance to tie him over which June thought this was very decent of the old man.

"Don't know how I lost it…I hadn't much to drink or anything…wasn't that I was out of it…I remember having my wallet when we left the pub…we went back to a friend's house to play cards…I don't know must have dropped it on the way home…" He was very distraught his rent was due and he wouldn't be able to meet the payment.

"May all your bad luck go with it…" June felt sorry for him and offered him money to pay his rent he could pay her back when he had it. The offer was gladly accepted wasn't as if she was spending much these days. A good book and a cup of tea and she was content for the night.

The morning had dragged even more than usual June looked at the piece of paper with her mother's number on it, almost illegible now and told herself she was going to call that number again she would go to Tilly's on her way home.

"Here it goes." She dialled the number this time putting a zero where she had previously put an eight. It rang and rang she wanted to hang up yet waited for the next ring, "Hello…"

She froze, couldn't speak for a moment "Valerie?"

"Yes, this is Valerie…who's this?"

"Valerie…its June…"

There was a silence then a sob, "oh my God…June…you rang…"

There was another long silence. "I've waited so long…oh my God…"

June asked if maybe they could meet up for a chat as Valerie continued to sob at the other end of the line.

Walking towards the coffee shop on the corner next day Valerie felt sick.

What should I say to her? she'd thought to herself.

"I mustn't frighten her off…" She was trembling as she took her handkerchief out of her bag.

The coffee shop was nice and quiet there was no one to notice her anxiety.

She hadn't slept, her mind racing with the excitement of seeing her daughter again. She had fretted about what she would wear.

She wanted to give the right impression.

June didn't know what to expect in meeting her mother she had thought about it for so long and had been so disappointed with the previous phone call.

She hadn't slept very well either the new neighbours had kept her awake with screaming and shouting coming from the house, Walter's old house.

It was scary and it hadn't been the first time.

Yet they would appear the following morning as if nothing had happened, the dad would walk past her window taking the children to school the mam waving them off from the gate. June was sure there was something strange about that family something very strange. She felt for the children she was sure they would have heard the goings-on too.

She hoped he wasn't cruel to them the mam was very distant June would often say hello in passing but she always held her head down.

It wasn't the house it used to be when Walter and Lily lived there or even when Lily had passed on Walter had kept the house spotless now it looked neglected. The dad all spruced up as if he'd just stood down from a bandbox the mam wore an apron with her hair tied back in a ponytail.

June would have loved to make friends with her but she didn't seem to mix with anyone around, *it would have been hard moving into a new neighbourhood* she'd thought *not knowing anyone.*

It had to be lonely for her with the children gone to school and the dad at work. Maybe she would call by some time with a pie or something. On her way to meet her mother June decided to call on Greta.

"Come in a girl…you're drenched…" Greta was so delighted to see June.

"Goodness…it's brutal out there…" June wanted to talk to her about going to meet her mother she remembered she had mentioned her before although briefly, but she always thought Greta knew a bit more.

Delighted to hear that she was meeting her mother Greta thought to herself it was an ideal opportunity to come clean and tell June she had been in touch with her mother all along. Since their chats had become more frequent, she always felt she was keeping something from her not in a bad way just there never seemed to be the appropriate moment to mention it. She would tell her today.

"…you must have smelled the tea…" She laughed as she took June's umbrella and left it standing in the sink.

"June. I…I…have something to tell you love…I should have told you a long time ago…" As the story unfolded amid tears and tea sipping Greta told her everything. How as teenagers her mother and herself would have such laughs going to the dances and teasing the boys, all very innocent. Lovely memories frozen in the midst of time. When she met up with Roger or Red as they used to call him it was just as friends Greta had thought until she realised Valerie was carrying his child. Seemingly Valerie hadn't told her friend the whole story they had been seeing each other on the quiet, him being married and all. She had kept it a secret until she started to show and then it all came out.

"…your grandmother was livid…as much as your mother tried to convince her that they were in love…she never accepted it…the shame of it…she was livid…"

Going on to talk about the tragedy that would end Roger's life Greta said she did believe that they were truly in love albeit under the wrong circumstances.

"…Roger had married for the wrong reasons they used to say…trapped in a loveless marriage…some would say he was scarred…damaged…though…I don't know…love unreturned…maybe…who knows…life is strange June…and love even more complex…"

June didn't know whether to be cross with her for not telling her all of this sooner or to be grateful that she had told her at all this was her father she was talking about, it can't have been easy. She watched as Greta awaited her reaction to being told, would she hold this against her? Had she spoiled their friendship?

She so appreciated spending time with June, it had put her in mind of the times she had spent with her mother in days gone by she had many of her traits and she hoped she hadn't ruined it but she had to tell her. Especially now she was going to meet up with her mother. June thanked her for telling her and told her she had appreciated that it couldn't have been easy.

"…sure…I'm a long-time a girl wanting to tell you…but I didn't know where to start…I knew you had a number for Valerie she'd told me…and I knew she wanted you to ring her so much…but it had to be your decision…it was an awful fix to be in altogether…I hope you can forgive me June…I wouldn't want you to stop calling or anything…"

June assured her that she would call by as usual and nothing would change between them and she was off. Valerie would be waiting.

Greta breathed a sigh of relief it was like a load off her mind the sheer weight of it was bringing her down at times.

As June approached the coffee shop and opened the door her heart was beating so fast that she was sure that the waitress who had just passed her by could hear it.

She was so excited and fearful at the same time this day could change her whole life she might not be alone anymore.

No words said they embraced silently and then laughed as June's elbow tipped over the vase of flowers on the table.

"I am so happy to see you…" and through the tears Valerie continued.

"I grieve for the years I have lost with you…and you know…the world doesn't stop for your grief…there comes a time…when you have to turn the page…I thought I had lost you forever."

June could see her mother was ecstatic why hadn't she rung that number ages ago so much wasted time.

Valerie had continued to work as a housekeeper and lived in on a small wage for many years she'd tried hard to get a place of her own and now lived in a council flat not far from town. She'd wished she could have done something better with her life something her daughter could be proud of. She was working as a seamstress now working from home doing repairs didn't pay much but it paid the bills.

"…you are the only thing in my life that I can be proud of…I have missed you for so long…" She took her daughter's hand in hers and squeezed it tightly.

"…yet in my heart we meet every day."

"…no wedding ring I see." They laughed and June began to tell her about Matt.

"He was the love of my life…my soul mate…that half of you that makes you whole…you know…" June welled up it was all too much.

"I will never love anyone as much as I have loved Matt…" It was the first time she had said that to anyone the first time she had even admitted it to herself. Maybe there was a connection after all a mother and daughter thing that opens your heart to one another there had been an intense moment of belonging that she had never felt before, a familiarity that filled her with joy.

As she sat on the bus home she slowly began to realise that things would never be the same again it would take time but then we are none of us harmonious in the symphony of life. We all have to adjust at times, adapt to different situations it may take a lifetime to get to know oneself depending on what an individual has been exposed to.

Today she had tea with her mother who knows what tomorrow might bring.

The bus stopped outside the baker's shop today there were road works and the driver apologised that he would have to drop them off a bit before the bus stop. Looking in the window of the shop June thought she might buy a nice pie and drop it into the new neighbours.

Chapter 3

The children would be back from school soon and it would be a nice treat for them. She knocked on the door and waited and waited and just as she was about to go the door opened just enough to see who was standing there, or at least her nose.

"Hi…I'm June…just live up the road…wanted to welcome you to the neighbourhood." And she held the pie out to her.

She was very young close up much younger than the husband or partner she wasn't sure. She opened the door slightly wider and took the pie in both hands.

"Thank you…you're very kind…" June hoped to have a little chat but not today. As she handed her the pie, June noticed a cigarette burn on her wrist. She recognised the burn as she had seen it so many times on the hands of Mrs Carey's grandson. He was such a troubled boy who was into self-harming as he became a teenager. Seeing the expression on June's face the girl retrieved into the hallway very quickly and closed the door. That poor girl June thought what kind of a life was she putting up with. There was nothing she could do coming home after being with her mother she was struggling to suppress her elation she wanted to do good for somebody and pass on the good feeling but instead she was left feeling deflated. Walking home she thought about Mrs Carey's grandson she wondered what he was at these days she remembered the day the post office had been broken into a while ago now. Poor Mac, he'd gotten such a roasting from the guards.

She was convinced Mrs Carey's grandson had done the deed but it was never proven hearing about his troubles and how he had been in and out of correction centres since then she was truly convinced it had been him.

Water under the bridge now.

Greta was standing at the gate as she walked by.

"How did it go?" She had obviously been watching for the bus but June explained to her that they had been dropped off way down the road because of the roadworks.

"…what in the name of Moses are they digging for again…I think myself they must be digging for gold…there's always a hole being dug somewhere…" June had to laugh, Greta had lightened the moment she would maybe see her new neighbour again and try to befriend her she wouldn't give up she looked like she needed a friend.

Greta with eyes wide open listened attentively as June spoke about her meeting with Valerie.

"June…I am so delighted for the pair of you…you know…your mother…had sadly resigned herself to…aw sure no point dwelling on the past."

Greta was humming to herself as she filled the kettle to make a cup of tea.

"I was just thinking…family are not always friends you know June…take mine for instance." Greta went on to talk about the somewhat complex characters that made up her own family.

Along with a curious chain of events that had taken place by her brother.

"God be good to him…" She had said blessing herself three times and looking up to the heavens. "…squatted in a council house with only drink as his companion to be found curled up in a corner… dead for three days they'd said…

"…and sure he didn't have a drinking problem you know…it was us that had the problem…and us losing sleep at night worrying about him…" Greta went on to talk about her sister who had set fire to her house to claim the insurance with a plan to elope and live-in luxury, which didn't go according to plan.

"…crackpots the lot of them…families…I won't go on lovey…could write a book…"

June had no idea, in looking at Greta one would never realise her background had been anything like as distressing as it sounded, she always had a smile.

She hadn't gone into any more detail but June could see there was a lot more to tell. "I will be meeting Valerie again at the weekend…why don't you come along?" Greta thanked her but thought it better to let them get to know each other a bit more and then they could all have a coffee together maybe.

"…sounds good…you know Greta…I could see a lot of sadness in her eyes…is there anything going on…I mean…we only talked about this and that…didn't get into any deep conversations or anything…it's just…I don't know…she looked kinda sad at times…?"

"I'm sure everything's fine lovey…give her time…give her time…"

Now June was really worried walking home she had herself convinced that Greta was keeping something from her as well, it was the way she had got up from the table and stood with her back to her at the sink like she didn't want to face her. She would have to wait if her mother had something to tell her she was sure she would.

Mr Oakley was in a foul mood even worse than usual. Aidan tipped her off as she got into work just as well she was on time, she thought!

Mrs Sheridan was all on for a big chat as she signed for her pension at the counter. "You'll never guess what June…you'll never guess…"

Aware that she was being watched by a pair of beady eyes from behind his glasses June ignored her boss.

"What is it Mrs Sheridan…don't tell me you won the sweep…"

"…aw no such luck dear…it's Cheeky…he's a she…he's a she June…went out this morning and there she was with her beautiful kittens…my goodness…what a surprise I got…" June wondered how she could have had the cat for so long and not know it was a female but obviously she didn't. She was delighted.

"…pop in if you're passing…they're so cute…" June promised her she would and off she went like the cat that got the cream.

Mr Oakley cleared his throat loudly and June got on with her work. Having arranged to meet up with her mother again June made her way to the coffee shop.

Valerie looked lovely as she walked towards the door June thought, she had got there early and was just thinking it might be nice to invite her to dinner sometime, cook something nice for her.

It was easier to chat now the awkwardness had passed, she wondered if perhaps it was a bit soon to delve into her private life although she was eager to know. The conversation as before was kept very light, perhaps it was too soon.

They would meet up again.

Aidan had reported the loss of his wallet to the guards to no avail. As he handed June the money she had lent to him he thanked her for her help and would never forget her for getting him out of a spot. She wondered about Milly's job she would love to have seen Aidan in a better job than he was. She told him about the position that was coming available and asked if he would be interested. He was a genius with figures, on the very rare occasion even Mr Oakley would complement him on his work (on the very rare occasion!).

That job would suit him perfectly. Milly was so excited to hear June's voice on the phone she'd thought June herself might have decided to go for it and hearing it was Aidan she hesitated a bit but said she would put in a good word for him. June assured her he had come highly recommended. She wasn't doing Mr Oakley any favours and would probably have to put up with his moods until he'd found some other misfortunate but it would be worth it.

Aidan would be the next bookkeeper at the Old Forge, it was confirmed.

He'd smiled right through his two weeks' notice and was replaced by Agnes a retired bank clerk who as it turned out would put Mr Oakley back into his box very swiftly. Calm, assertive and quite capable Agnes had the sort of face one couldn't put an age on perhaps June thought to herself she had retired for a reason. She certainly didn't look old enough to be of retirement age.

It was funny to see the pair of them in action Mr Oakley going out of his way to accommodate his new employee almost jumpy in her presence.

"Want a cup of tea Jane?" June had told her umpteen times her name was June but she still insisted on calling her Jane.

"That would be nice..." June left her desk to join her companion.

"...put the kettle on there so...good girl...it'll be boiled by the time you run to the bakery and get a couple of scones...love them when they're fresh..."

Agnes didn't even lift her head from the books as she spoke.

June smiled to herself. She certainly was a bit of a character.

"Oh! ...and don't be getting the ones with the currants in them...they stick to my false teeth...they're a curse..." Still looking into her books Agnes continued...

"...I remember my father used to say...there's currants for cakes and raisins for everything..."

June was giggling walking down the road it was nice to have a bit of normal company around she thought, Mr Oakley had truly met his match in Agnes for sure.

Meeting her mother again wasn't as scary as the first time although still a little bit so.

As she entered the coffee shop, June waved at her but today, she wasn't alone.

"Hi June...this is my partner Joe..."

June shook hands feeling a bit in the dark why hadn't she mentioned him before, she had been right in suspecting there was more to be unveiled regarding her mother, it had been so many years sure there had to be.

Joe got up to go as she sat down, "…he's working on the building site around the corner…just came in to wait with me…I wanted you to meet him…I hope that's ok?" Valerie looked worried and hoped it hadn't been too soon to introduce her partner she was after all still getting to know her daughter.

"Not at all…it's lovely to meet you, Joe." They shook hands and he was off on his way.

"We've been together now for about fifteen years…goodness time flies…he's very good to me…even on hearing about my sad existence that was my past he stuck by me."

"I am so happy for you Valerie…you deserve any happiness you can find…and you're lucky to have found…someone…" June hesitated as she thought of her own sad existence, would she ever love again?

Turned out Joe had had an interesting past as well but that was for another day.

Next morning there was shouting as she approached the post office door Agnes was giving out to Mr Oakley about her chair.

"You try sitting on it for eight hours in the day you'd be humped by the time you get up out of it…it must be forty-years-old."

June passed in and said nothing, seeing her pass by Agnes invited her into the conversation.

"What do you think Jane…is this antique only fit for the dump or what?"

After a lot of huffing and puffing from Mr Oakley, Agnes got her new chair next day and all was well again.

"Now…that's better." She sat back comfortably as she continued.

"I'm bad enough besides sitting crooked all day…sure he must have his communion money…didn't spend much on this place anyway."

June was enjoying her company even if it was letting off steam a lot of the time at least she had a bit of nature in her. Having invited Valerie for tea June waited anxiously as she came up the path.

"Come in…you're welcome…" June stood aside as Valerie slowly walked past her in the hallway.

"This brings me back…" Valerie had tears in her eyes as she walked into the kitchen. Probably much the same as the day she'd left, June hadn't done much to the old house Pop used to maintain it well and she liked the old furniture and stuff, didn't see the need to modernise.

"…here sit down." As June pulled the chair out at the table Valerie sat down.

Not wanting to make too much of a fuss she had decided to do a nice salad for the tea after waking early tormenting herself as to what to make *Maybe a roast* she'd thought, but she wouldn't have the time after work she liked to cook a roast slowly. It was the way Nan always did it then she'd thought perhaps chicken but that too would be a rush. In the end, after nearly giving herself a headache she settled for a nice bit of ham and a salad.

It seemed to go down well Valerie spoke for a while about her memories of the place while June followed closely as she took a trip down memory lane.

"…you know June…even after all those years it's like slipping into an old comfortable pair of shoes…there's such a welcoming feeling about the place."

There was a sadness about her as she looked at the old photographs on the mantelpiece some of Nan and Pop and some of June.

"…I should have fought for you June…I have missed so much…but there were so many…" Valerie excused herself and asked where the toilet was.

"…are you ok?" June put a hot drop of tea in her half-filled cup as she returned from the toilet.

"…you know the story June…I'm sure my mother painted a good picture of all that went on…I was young…so young…I was afraid…don't ask me what I was afraid of…but I was so afraid and ashamed…I was stupid…really stupid…

"I know now that it was wrong…that my mother was wrong…but back in those days…well…it was the shame really…they couldn't look me in the eye…brought it all on myself though…if the truth be known!"

Valerie went on to say that she had caused so much hurt and humiliation she thought it best to stay away.

"…I know it's a bit late to be giving my daughter advice…but one thing I will say to you June…and I'm talking from experience…there are many roadblocks in life…don't be like me…if you reach a wall don't turn round…find a way to climb over it."

They talked for hours seems Valerie had met Joe when he came to visit his aunt who happened to be the lady she was keeping house for.

They'd got on well from the start and started going out shortly after they'd met.

When he'd called the first time his aunt had gone into detail of how he had been 'interfered with' as she had put it. She'd kept it to herself for so long, she'd carried it as a burden. Finally it came out and there was no more said on the matter.

They had been a long time going out together before Joe had mentioned this embarrassingly as though it had been something he had done wrong. She too would keep her promise to his aunt and say nothing.

It had stolen his childhood, left him cowardly and nervous one could almost say he was disturbed growing up and only he knew why. It only came out at his aunt's house when she promised not to tell anybody if he'd tell her why he was always so anxious. Right or wrong at the time she'd kept her promise.

"…even in his sleep…he still cries out…" Valerie got up to go.

June was hardly able to take in what she was after hearing she'd often heard of stuff like this going on but had never known anyone who had suffered it.

It had made her shiver. It had been a late night and June was tired the next day.

Agnes came through the door of the post office with a basin in her hand and not wanting to be rude June just bid her good morning and passed no remarks.

"Will you put the kettle on there Jane…there's a good girl…my bunion is killing me…I brought the Epsom salts…thought I might steep the old feet for a while."

You could expect anything with Agnes June thought to herself, nothing would surprise her at this stage.

"…wait now until I see…don't want it too hot because I'm bad enough without having blisters as well…aw that's lovely…oh! t'is heaven…"

She only had her feet in the basin when Mr Oakley walked in.

"…wouldn't be coming over here now Mr O…not if you want to enjoy your pickled onions again…I have bunions as big as marbles…"

Mr Oakley didn't know where to look she had her skirt pulled up around her exposing the white lace of her bloomers June had never seen him go in and out so fast. She had given up on asking her to call her June and not Jane!

Valerie had spent the afternoon going through her old photographs she had arranged to meet June at the bus station and they would come back to hers for a cup of tea. There it was the one photo she had been looking for!!!

June had such a likeness to him except for the hair she hadn't inherited the red hair.

"You were beautiful…I mean…" June got a bit embarrassed she didn't mean she wasn't beautiful still but she really was a beauty back then.

"That's ok love…time replaces youth with wisdom…not sure I'm any wiser though." And they laughed.

Valerie handed her the photo of herself and Roger her dad, June gasped to see the likeness all along and in listening to Greta she was sure she looked like her mother. She had her hair colour but that was all it made her longing more intense to have known her dad.

"…tell me about him." She wasn't sure if it was the right time but her mother had just handed her his picture she must be ready to talk.

If anything was evident from their conversation it was that they were a couple infatuated with each other Valerie's features softened as she spoke about him. It was like for a few moments the pain that was lining her middle-aged face had vanished and June began to feel her pain. How did she cope, she had no one not even her family she wasn't sure she would have coped very well under the circumstances herself?

"…you must feel so much resentment…I don't understand…Nan and Pop…they were such good people…why would…could they do that to their only daughter…I don't understand it…" Valerie took her daughter's hand in hers and held it for a few minutes.

"…look…no use in dragging up the past eh!" Valerie put the photographs back in the box and smiled.

"…who was it that said 'An eye for an eye only leaves everybody blind.' I remember hearing that somewhere…and it's true…it does no good."

She took the photo of herself and Roger out of the box again and handed it to June. "Would you like to have it?"

June took the photo and thanked her it had been both an enlightening and heart-breaking evening but she felt she was getting to know her mother a little bit more every time they met it was never going to be all sunshine and flowers, such is life.

Just clearing up after breakfast June stretched and yawned and wished it was the weekend, as she walked to the hallway to pick up the post there was a ring at the door.

"Hi…" She was surprised and delighted to see her new neighbour at the door with her little girl holding on to her apron.

"…hello you…what's your name?" June stooped down to the little girl.

"I'm sorry to bother you…but could I borrow a jug of milk…I…"

Looking embarrassed her neighbour held an empty jug out to June.

"…of course you can…come into the kitchen I'm just after getting up from the table…there you go…and there's no need to return it." June handed her a full bottle of milk from the fridge.

"…I'm Maddie…and this is Sarah…say hello Sarah…" She reached behind her to bring the little girl forward but she dug even more into her apron.

"…she's a bit shy…thank you so much…I will return it…dropped my last bottle taking it out of the fridge…thank you."

Chapter 4

"…oh! …goodness…I hope you didn't cut yourself…" June was genuinely concerned and only too happy to help she was so glad now that she'd called by with the pie it had broken the ice. She might not have called for the milk if she hadn't introduced herself that day and maybe the children would have to go to school hungry. It was a good feeling helping someone out like that, a really good start to the day.

When she returned home that evening there was a bottle of milk left on her doorstep and two homemade scones.

She smiled to herself and thought what a lovely thing to do it's the little things that count.

Wasn't long before she had befriended the children as well. The husband or partner she wasn't sure which, seemed a bit distant though.

Sarah was the youngest little girl Heidi the middle child and Sam the oldest.

She'd heard Maddie address the dad as Dan but had not been introduced.

Rooting through her drawer June was sure she had a frame somewhere, she would frame the photograph of her dad and Valerie though she thought to herself Nan would probably turn in her grave if she saw it on the mantelpiece.

It looked rather good in the old silver frame as she sat and looked at it for a while they'd made a lovely couple or rather they would have under the right circumstances. She wondered if things had been different where she might be now, and would Roger have been a good dad. *He did have a look of kindness about him,* she thought. She felt a bit cheated not having had the chance to meet him or get to know him she had always thought of Pop as her dad and he was the best but she wondered if there would have been a different connection with her real dad. She would never know now.

Greta was so excited to hear about the old photographs and the chats she'd had with Valerie "You know June…I should have some old photo's too…somewhere…maybe I'll root them out…you might like to see them…?"

June promised to call by again soon and would look forward to seeing them.

Valerie had mentioned going to the graveyard and taking some flowers and asked June if she would go with her.

"It's funny…I miss them so much although sent packing…I never stopped loving them…it's too late now…I can never get that time back again…"

A tear came down her face as she leaned over the headstone and placed a kiss on first her mother's name and then her father's.

June was deeply touched and reached for her hand as she missed her step and began to stumble; she was physically shaking.

How could they have shut her out their own daughter it dn't seem right.

Was there more to the story? Maybe. Would she ever know the full story? Maybe never.

As she linked her mother out of the graveyard June turned as she always did and waved back at them, her Nan and her Pop and of course Walter and Lily.

The most important people in her childhood years now lying in the cold earth and she thought of Matt.

"I remember walking down this road…feeling empty…like I'd left a part of me behind." Valerie sat on the wall outside the graveyard as if exhausted by the experience she stared into the ground and she looked pale. June hoped she was ok she really knew nothing about this woman she was a stranger to her.

She continued "…it was raining…had been raining for days…I used to tell myself…oh!… listen to me going on…I'm sure it's the last thing you want to hear…"

She got up to go but June told her to sit for a while and that she would love to hear all about it.

"…I used to tell myself…the rain bore a visible resemblance…to the terrible pain that fell drop by drop onto my heart…my mind was a torment to me…for a very long time." June felt sorry for her although she could not empathise with her not knowing the full story.

But today she thought maybe she was about to talk to her at last. They made their way back to the house and June sat her down for a nice cup of tea.

"…tell me about your life growing up June…I have missed so much…did they ever speak of me…your Nan and Pop I mean?"

June wanted to tell her that she had missed her every day but the truth was that she didn't she wanted to tell her that her Nan and Pop had talked about her all the time but they dn't.

The very rare mention of her name had come from her Pop who was instantly hushed by her Nan.

"Tell me Valerie…why? …what would cause such…I don't know…resentment…hatred…why did they never mention you? …and the birthday cards…why would they have been returned? …surely they would have appreciated your remembering me."

June wished she had asked Nan why all the bitterness? What was so bad that it was beyond forgiveness? But it was too late now.

Valerie got up to walk around the kitchen looking at the photographs as she walked.

"…I never really got on with my mother, June…growing up I mean…we were always at loggerheads…Dad would take my side then and there'd be sparks flying…" Valerie looked thoughtful. "…Dad would wink at me and it would be forgotten…but your nan…boy could she hold a grudge…sometimes I think although we were like chalk and cheese…I might have inherited her stubbornness…"

In listening to her reminisce June could see that Valerie had a completely different childhood to hers she'd had no time for her Nan whatsoever by the sounds of it, she talked for hours about her carefree teenage years drinking and staying out half the night. The good old days she called them.

Sounded to June like she had been a nightmare as a teenager.

"…I know…I know…you're thinking it's no wonder I was sent packing…I wasn't a fit mother…and you would be spot on in thinking that…I was a selfish waste of space…and my mother knew that."

"...she'd had your best interests at heart June when she packed my bags."

The tea had gone cold as June sat with her mouth open listening, not believing half of what she was hearing her mouth was dry.

The doorbell rang and Valerie looked at her watch.

"...I'd better be off anyway June...we'll talk again ok love?"

She was off down the road and June wasn't sure if she wanted to hear anymore. Her precious memories of her Nan and Pop the two people that meant the world to her were being mutilated and she wasn't about to let that happen.

The postman stood at the door holding a parcel and as June took it from him she thanked him. She wondered who would be sending her a parcel.

Clodagh hoped it was ok to take the liberty of sending on some of her stuff, the letter attached and addressed to June explained how she planned on coming home and wanted to lighten her load. She would be arriving at the end of the month. June hurriedly went to make up the bed the parcel must have been two weeks coming there were two days left before the end of the month.

Assuming Clodagh would stay with her for a while at least she went about changing the bedclothes and put a hot water bottle into the bed.

It had been a while since anyone had slept in it and it needed airing.

She hoovered the room and put a nice vase of flowers on the dresser to welcome her. June was so excited to see her old friend again that she could hardly wait. So much had changed since she'd seen her last so much to catch up on. She hoped she was returning for good this time.

Clodagh looked drawn and tired the journey had apparently taken a lot out of her.

"Oh! it's so good to see you." June hugged her friend as she came up the garden path.

"It's good to be home." Clodagh had felt her time was done in Africa she had worked really hard but enjoyed every minute of it and would do it again if her health hadn't let her down. Since the malaria she had never really recovered her full strength. She had found it hard the last couple of years and it showed in her face.

"…you were great to go out there at all…" June carried her bag into the house and left it by the stairs, "…you'll be staying for a while I hope…I've made up the bed?"

Clodagh smiled, "…dear June…you are so kind…and as usual…so generous but no I have arranged to stay with my aunt…you remember Daisy? …she's getting on a bit…so we'll be company for each other." June couldn't hide her disappointment. "…but if it's ok I will stay tonight…don't know what time the busses go…and I don't think I have the energy to even go and check it out now."

Relieved that she would be able to spend a little time with her friend June smiled and made her feel at home.

"…sure, you're as welcome as the day is long…"

They chatted well into the early hours Clodagh couldn't believe Mac had moved on from the post office he'd had so many plans for it when she sold it to him. She was glad to hear that June still had a job there though.

It had been over a week since she had called to see Greta so June decided she would call on the way home. Cheerful as ever she was delighted to see her.

"I'm after hanging out the wash and what happens when I turn my back? ...the line broke...come in a girl it's so nice to see you...how are things?"

June wanted to ask Greta about Valerie there was something she hadn't told her she was sure of it and it was bugging her.

Still walking down the hallway into the kitchen Greta continued to talk as June followed behind.

"...I found those photos...remember the ones I was telling you about...last time I saw you...wait now a minute...where did I put them? ...sure my head is gone...here they are." She took an envelope from behind an ornament on the sideboard and handed it to June.

"...wasn't she a beauty?" She pointed to Valerie who really was a beauty in those days. Still holding on to her looks though a bit ragged looking now June thought.

"We went to the cemetery last week...went round to all the graves..." June looked through the photographs and stopped to look at one with a group of people in it.

"...that's me...seems like a hundred years ago now...aw! ...the fun we had." Greta was thoughtful as she fiddled with the clothes peg she was still holding since she was hanging the clothes out, while looking over June's shoulder.

"...this one here I remember it well...your father...God rest the poor man...took that...see your mother is expecting you in this one...I remember that dress...she made it herself...couldn't afford to be buying new clothes back then...you either took out the old sewing machine and added a bit of width…or made something yourself…she was a good hand at the sewing…your mother."

"…Greta…we had a long chat that day…after the cemetery I mean…she didn't get along with Nan…did she?" June hoped she wasn't speaking out of turn.

"…your grandmother was a wonderful woman…putting up with a lot she made a good job of rearing you June…and they were hard times…your mother well…don't know if it's my place…they were difficult times…"

Greta went on to say that Valerie had been her best friend from childhood and how she had spent many a day playing with her in her Nan's house.

How June's Nan would bake cakes and white soda bread and they would have black currant jam on it.

"…can still taste it…it was so good…you'd eat it all day if you got it."

June remembered the white soda bread herself that Nan used to bake pity she thought to herself that she hadn't picked up the talent herself.

"…seems Valerie had gotten into the wrong crowd," Greta said with a look in her eyes that made it believable. Going on to say that they had sort of drifted apart for a while, they would still go out occasionally but Valerie became very secretive didn't share her feelings or anything not like they used to.

"…I missed the closeness…to be honest…then I got used to it I suppose…"

She had begun to drink heavily staying out all night and began to have this couldn't care less attitude. Her whole personality changed overnight, Greta said.

"…your Nan was as patient as she could be with her…she would call to our house and ask if I'd seen her when she wouldn't come home of a night…"

Might be early morning Greta went on and she'd be in her nightgown at the door freezing half the time. June was beginning to understand why things had worked out the way they did, Greta was painting a very grim picture.

"…as sure as I'm standing here…your Nan did everything she could to help Valerie…and your Pop sure the poor man was bending over backwards to please her…when if you don't mind me saying so…a good kick in the backside is what she needed." Greta was getting vexed.

"…it's hard to help someone if they don't want to help themselves June…you know lovey…it's very hard."

They talked for hours Valerie it seemed was having the time of her life without a care for anyone.

"…I hope I haven't said too much June…thinking back it just vexes me so much…your dad…Roger…he was a nice man…a drinker too but a moderate one."

As it turned out when Valerie realised she was expecting his baby she drank even more, Nan had warned her that if she didn't look after herself she would lose the baby. Valerie didn't seem to care but it was the drink Greta said.

"…your Nan told her she would look after her until the baby was born…even though back then it brought such shame…and once the baby was born she was on her own unless she gave up the drinking…she told her straight."

Valerie had gone on a binge for three days after Roger was found dead had got into trouble with the guards for damaging property while under the influence and it was all too much, when she got home from the guard's station her mother had her bags packed and waiting for her at the door. She'd found her a live-in job that would pay pittance but would pay for her keep and maybe she might sober up. The rest was history Greta had said.

"…your mother is a changed woman now though…she told me Joe had made her think on about her lifestyle…even though she had gone on drinking for a long time after they met… I told you how they'd met, didn't I? …or did I? sure my head is gone…I do be telling people things over and over again…old age a girl."

Seems Valerie had continued to drink long after she'd met Joe wasn't earning much in her cleaning job but Joe ever the gentleman wouldn't hear of a lady paying her way. This of course suited Valerie down to the ground.

She would sneak into her bedroom late at night so as not to awaken the old lady now frail and every day more dependent on people. Mostly Joe he was such a good nephew went out of his way to be kind to her and had never let her down. The morning he'd found her having passed away peacefully in her sleep he'd also found Valerie asleep on the toilet having spent the night throwing up, intoxicated from the night before.

Dragging her back to her room he'd wondered how she could still be under the influence of drink they'd had a few but not that much the night before. It wasn't long before the mystery was solved empty bottles under her bed the cheapest alcohol you could buy. Poison and nothing surer he was furious didn't know whether to be angry with her or to pity her settling after a lot of thought for the latter.

Greta had arranged to meet her in town that day and when she hadn't turned up she was worried so she called to the house and Joe had let her in.

He'd explained how he'd found his poor aunt and then found Valerie almost unconscious from drink.

It had been a wake-up call for Valerie she'd promised never to touch the stuff again and she hadn't.

Joe had kept her on and continued to pay her for the housekeeping until it became embarrassing, she'd got herself a nice little flat and seemed to get her life in order. Joe had been and continued to be her rock.

June knew there had been some dark secret lurking there each time she had met with her mother maybe one day she would tell her or maybe not!

Greta jumped up from the table. "…would you look at the pest…get out…get out!" She ran with the tea towel to chase Mrs Sheridan's cat out of the back garden. Disappearing over the wall with a pair of her best stockings.

"…well that cat…he'll be the cause of my death yet…puts my blood pressure up…came in the window one day and helped himself to a bit of liver I was only after frying…" Greta wiped her forehead with the tea towel she was carrying.

"…only had my back turned for a minute to pour a drop of tea…and there he was gone off for himself with my lovely bit of lamb's liver…don't know does she feed him at all?"

June had to laugh. "…he's actually a she…Greta…just had kittens!"

When the alarm clock rang June had to drag herself out of the bed, she felt both physically and mentally exhausted. Her thoughts on what Greta had told her had shone a different light on her mother it all seemed so unreal like something she'd read about in a magazine. It was a lot to take in and she was a bit apprehensive now about meeting Valerie after work.

Clodagh went on her way and promised not to be a stranger and June wished her well and promised her the same.

Mr Oakley had fallen over a box and Agnes was trying to lift him on to the chair when June got in to work.

"Oh!…thank goodness…lend us a hand here Jane…there's a good girl it's like lifting a beached whale…now…Mr O…you need to be more careful…falling over boxes at your age…you'll be killing yourself…man…"

June thought he looked a bit pale and went to get him a drink of water he thanked her and smiled, it was the first time he had been civil with her since she started working there. She thought to herself maybe she hadn't done much either to be friendly with him but she was half afraid of him. Looking at him being hauled onto the chair he looked old and vulnerable not one to be afraid of it was very hard to put an age on him but she reckoned he was way up there.

"Isn't your name June?" Mr Oakley looked a bit puzzled.

"Yes Mr Oakley…but Agnes insists on calling me Jane." They both laughed and as if he in a split second he realised who he was talking to his face changed from a smile to his usual stern look and he cleared his throat and got up to go.

"Do you know but I think Mr O might needs to change his glasses…that box was there clear as day and over he went and fell over it…I only left it there for a minute…was thinking it was a nice size for storing the old newspapers."

June had settled in behind her desk and Agnes was still talking.

Chapter 5

"…went to get a newspaper just to check the size…and if he didn't walk in and fall over it…squashed it into the bargain…I don't know this is no good to anyone now…I do keep the newspapers for starting the fire you know…they're great for starting the fire…" Agnes was all a fluster.

As the bus pulled up outside the coffee shop June had promised herself to take each day as it came each meeting with Valerie as it unfolded and definitely not to judge.

"I must apologise…for our last conversation…I must have left you thinking…well…I wouldn't blame you for what you think now…and that was only the tip of the iceberg." Valerie had a quiver in her voice and it all came out!

"…I went off the rails June for a long time…paid for it one hundred-fold…lost my family…lost you…I was a mess." She went on to talk for nearly an hour nonstop it was like she was trying to offload a huge burden sighing with relief in conclusion leaving her as if wiped out. She hid nothing told it exactly as Greta had, left nothing out June could now empathise with her after all she didn't harbour any glamorous illusions regarding meeting her mother now they could maybe get to know each other without any false pretence.

"To know all is to forgive all." Pop used to say that.

In a weird sort of way June felt a bit of relief as well going there on the bus she had been thinking all kinds of things rehearsing all kinds of questions she might ask her mother but as it turned out she needn't have worried. She slept on the way home on the bus could only have been for a few minutes but had she not been awoken at her stop she would have to walk a long way back again.

Dan, her new neighbour had awoken her as he got up to get off at the stop himself. "Think this is our stop."

June jumped and walked in a state of stupor off the bus.

"…I'm so sorry…I hope I didn't startle you…I have seen you get off at this stop before." *He looked very apologetic and genuine*, June thought.

"Not at all…I dosed for a minute…long day…thank you…thanks."

She walked ahead but could feel him walk closely behind for some reason or other he always gave her the creeps.

"…it's a lovely neighbourhood here we love it …" Catching up on her he was now walking beside her making conversation, he actually seemed very nice. Maybe she had judged him wrongly though she was usually a very good judge of character but she would give him the benefit of the doubt for now.

As they turned the corner to the street where they both lived, Dan's two little girls came running towards them lifting the smallest one up in his arms, he took Heidi the other little girl by the hand.

"Mummy is sad." Sarah the youngest little girl mumbled to her dad as she sucked her thumb. Dan assured her everything would be ok and as they turned into their gate, June bid them goodbye. Maybe she had been wrong about Dan just she always thought there was something not right about this couple she remembered how Matt would tickle her and tell her not to be reading into things she had a habit of taking on the worries of the world he would say.

Valerie was waiting outside the post office when June came out for her lunch break the following day. She was surprised to see her they hadn't arranged to meet or at least she didn't think so.

"Hi…" She greeted her mother with a smile.

"Hi June…I hope you don't mind me turning up like this without making arrangements."

Valerie looked sort of dressed up, June thought.

"…not at all…it's nice to see you…you off somewhere nice? …I mean you look like you're going somewhere." Looking at her admiringly June thought to herself how she looked so much younger dressed up.

"…oh! …this old thing…no I just said I'd get a wear out of it." Valerie had thought maybe it would be nice to surprise her and take her for a bit of lunch somewhere. June although a teensy-weensy bit suspicious agreed that it would be lovely.

They picked up a couple of cakes from the bakery shop and sat by the quayside it was a beautiful day. For a while they both sat staring into the water as people went by busy with their own affairs. She was beginning to feel a bit closer to her mother now and every time they would meet up a little closer still. It was a strange sort of a feeling but very calming she felt almost tranquil in her presence.

She was beginning to realise how much she had missed out on in not being close to her growing up was it too late to bond now?

Was this a feeling of connecting somehow of bonding?

"…June you know I don't drink now…haven't for a long time…as you know…once an alcoholic always an alcoholic as they say…so I won't be drinking ever again." Valerie had a sincere look on her face.

"…if I had my time over again I would never touch the stuff …such a waste…"

June listened conscious of the time Mr Oakley would be looking at his watch at this stage.

"…I wondered if…well its totally up to yourself…but I was thinking of giving Joe a bit of a surprise party…he'll be sixty next month…what do you think…would you come?" Valerie was hesitant in asking and waited eagerly for her daughter's reply. June assured her that she would be there and indeed would be delighted to be there. It would only be a small affair Valerie went on, a couple of his mates from the building site and their wives just a little get together to mark the day. He would have a fit but he would enjoy it once he was over the shock. June apologised that she had to run that Mr Oakley would be humming and hawing for the afternoon if she was late.

Agnes winked at her as she came through the door.

"Take no notice dear…he's like a basket of cats…here have a biscuit they're my favourite…if only I had a knife and a bit of butter…two digestives with a bit of butter…mmm…nothing better." June didn't like to refuse but she didn't delay either. She had to be sitting behind her desk before Mr Oakley turned around. She took a biscuit and was sitting and looking busy as quickly as her legs could carry her. She thought about her lunch with her mother she hardly knew Joe, what would she get him for his birthday?

Mr Oakley excused himself and left for the afternoon he hadn't shut the door when Agnes was out of her seat.

" ...it's nice to stretch the old legs...you don't have that problem...you're too young...I get so stiff...one of these days I'm thinking I will seize up altogether..." June watched as Agnes helped herself to a sweet out of the jar.

"...I have a bit of a sweet tooth too." She walked over to where June was sitting.

"...Agnes...what would you buy for a gentleman that's sixty you know as a birthday present?"

Agnes put on her thoughtful face for a moment and June didn't know what to expect she could come out with anything.

"...well...that depends on how well you know this gentleman...you know what I mean." The thoughtful look had turned to a mischievous one.

"...you're of no help to me at all." June continued with her work and Agnes returned to her desk laughing.

Maybe a nice shirt June thought to herself or would that be too personal maybe a bottle of wine goodness no she thought no alcohol!

She would have to think of something maybe she would ask Greta.

Fr Mulcahy was on her heels as she passed by the chapel.

"T'is yourself June...and how are things with you...I see Valerie around the place... she was a difficult one...didn't think I'd ever lay eyes on her again in these parts." *Fr Mulcahy, well-known for sticking his nose in was barking up the wrong tree if he was looking for information from her*, June thought to herself.

"Oh...hello Fr...yes, all good with me...you'll be seeing a lot more of Valerie I think..." Leaving him with an even more curious look on his face she hurriedly crossed the road waving back at him so as not to appear rude.

"That fella…sure he's a right old busybody…take no notice of him at all."

Greta was delighted to see June at the door they had a laugh as she told her about Fr Mulcahy. "…he'll be going on and he'll strain his neck with all the looking he has out of that window…God forgive me and him a man of the cloth."

Valerie had invited Greta round to talk about the party for Joe and of course June would be there too they could discuss food and party stuff. She seemed all fired up about the occasion there wasn't a lot of money to spend on it but they would do a good job with what they had. Greta agreed to bake a nice cake maybe ice it too, Valerie was delighted. June would help her in paying for the foodstuff maybe they could do the shopping together.

As if timed all the party ideas had been discussed when Joe walked in.

"Sit down…I'll get you a cuppa…" Valerie was out of her chair before he'd taken his coat off. Adding more boiling water to the teapot she gave it a quick stir and poured him a cup of tea. Seemed a nice sort June thought, certainly didn't look sixty or coming up sixty. She chatted to Greta on the bus on the way back she too was having difficulty in deciding what to get him for a present.

"You know June…. I've known Joe for a good while…I remember when your mother started working for his aunt…I used to call to see her every now and then."

"…sure we'd do more arguing…stop…I was always trying to get her to call on your Nan…but sure one of them was every bit as stubborn as the other…it just wasn't to be…"

"...anyway ...poor Joe he was as quiet as a mousse don't know how he ever plucked up the courage to talk to her don't mind ask her out...I think it just happened...I think he took pity on her to be honest in the beginning."

"...she was a sorry state with the drink...t'is an ill wind that doesn't do someone good they say."

"...she used to say to me that Joe had put her on the right track...he'd shown so much concern for her...I don't know that it was ever a romantic relationship as such...now I could be wrong." Greta was thoughtful for a moment.

June walked her to her gate but didn't go in she'd been gone all day and hadn't done a thing in the house she wanted to do a bit of tidying up the breakfast things were still in the sink.

As she washed the dishes she thought of her Nan and how things could have been so different. She must have had regrets too Valerie was after all their only daughter, she had to have had.

She herself could hold no grudges against her mother; what was past was past she wasn't going to waste any more time, there had been more than enough time wasted already.

Walking by the old curiosity shop, June thought she would go in for a browse around she might see something for Joe's birthday. She thought it might be nice to get him something to show her appreciation for all he'd done to help her mother, sounded like he'd supported her through her roughest times. There was a brick a brack cabinet full to the brim with knickknacks, ornaments covered in dust and gadgets to beat the band. Nothing she thought to herself that would enhance one's existence. Closing the door behind her bidding the assistant a good day, though she was sure he was asleep behind the counter she spotted something in the window. It was a clock a simple mantle clock but it bore an inscription on the face written in gold.

"Thank you for taking the time."

It was perfect, she would go back in and ask about it. As she approached the counter the assistant did indeed appear to be sleeping an elderly gentleman she'd often browsed around the shop before but couldn't remember ever buying anything there. She excused herself and asked if she could see the clock but there was no response, she thought to herself she would call back later it wasn't as if it would be sold or anything didn't look like they were rushed off their feet by any means. As she stepped outside she had an awful thought.

"What if he'd passed away in his sleep behind the counter? Was he even breathing…she hadn't noticed…should she go back…check maybe?"

She was too afraid to go back but as she walked further down the road, she was afraid not to. Back she went her heart racing and not a sign of anyone around.

What would she do if he was dead? She would probably drop dead as well she was no good for anything like this but it was the right thing to do!

"Are you ok there miss? …my hearing aid must have fallen out never heard you come in…looking for anything in particular?"

June nearly jumped out of her skin he gave her the fright of her life but was she relieved.

He dusted off the clock and was more than happy to gift wrap it for her.

" …time…a thing of the past…people have no time now…too busy."

It must be a lonely life June thought waiting for a passer-by to drop in. She'd passed the door many times often seeing him stand there never thinking maybe a simple hello might have made his day. Next time she saw him she would make it her business to take the time to say hello.

It wasn't an expensive clock and nothing special but there was something about the inscription that had caught her eye she would show it to Valerie see what she'd think of it.

"It's perfect…really lovely…thank you June you needn't have…I'm sure Joe will love it." Valerie rubbed her finger over the inscription thoughtfully.

"…what do you think of this?" She hurriedly went to the cupboard and took out a coloured bag within the bag there was a box and in the box a beautiful necktie.

"…what do you think? …I bought it yesterday…he doesn't have a tie…I want him to look his best for the party." Valerie was glowing with excitement.

"…it's pure silk…a bit expensive but what harm…t'isn't every day you're sixty."

June took the tie and looked at it.

"It's beautiful…he'll love that…" as she handed it back to her mother, she noticed a shake in her hand.

She'd never noticed that before maybe it was the excitement. She almost felt sorry for her looking at the way she folded the tie so gently and with such love in her eyes she hoped Joe would appreciate it she was sure he would.

The party all organised all that was to do now was to make sure Joe wouldn't get wind of it and ruin the surprise there would be twenty-four people if everyone turned up. June wondered if it would be a tight squeeze in the flat she thought of maybe asking Valerie if she would like to hold the party back at her house. Although she appreciated the offer, Valerie wasn't sure Joe would feel comfortable about having it there. He was sort of set in his ways and he liked familiarity. They would be fine she would have the food stuff in the kitchen and have drinks in the little sitting room at the front.

June had never seen anyone so nervous as Valerie was on the night. She'd come early with Greta to help to set things up. It was just as well Valerie was about as useful as a bucket with a hole in it. June wondered if maybe having the drink around was having an effect on her it had to be a temptation even though it had been years. Something had her unsettled anyway Greta assured June there was no fear of her going near the stuff but best keep an eye on her just to be sure.

Joe had gone into work complaining of a sore back Valerie had joked that he'd soon be able to retire but he hadn't been amused she said.

She waited to give him his present when he'd get home. He could have a wash and get dressed up and wear his new tie she had ironed his best shirt.

He hadn't taken any notice of Greta and June being there when he got home, it was nothing out of the usual. Of course the party food had been left in the larder until he would go up for his wash and then it could be all set up.

Valerie handed him his present and he looked at her apologetically.

"I was a right old grump this morning…wasn't I? …sorry Val…" He opened his present and smiled.

"…you'll make a toff out of me yet…I love it, thank you…" He took it with him and was off up the stairs to have his wash.

Valerie looked so pleased and June was happy for her she had put a lot of thought into his present not to mention probably half of her week's wages.

Everybody turned up in a matter of minutes so that by the time Joe had changed and was indeed looking very smart in his shirt and tie there was a houseful and a very cheery 'Happy Birthday' sung. He was speechless turned to go but Valerie expecting as much walked him straight back into the room.

It was a lovely evening plenty of everything despite the worrying Valerie had put herself through in wondering if she'd got enough food.

As she watched Valerie watching Joe opening his present, June was so glad she'd found someone who cared so much for her perhaps even loved her.

Theirs seemed like such an easy relationship they seemed so comfortable in each other's company bound by all the awful memories of the past the booze and the anxieties that must have surrounded it, the rehabilitation the suffering that must have been attached to it. Now living a simple life Joe quietly strengthened Valerie and Valerie was beaming as if feeding on his strength. *There is strength in simplicity,* June thought to herself.

The clock got pride of place on the mantle alongside his new silk tie put back into the box maybe never to be worn again but with many happy memories packed away with it.

Mr Oakley was putting a sign in the window of the post office when June got into work, not wanting to seem nosey she would wait and read it when she went out for her lunch. Agnes was as usual full of the joys she had brought her knitting into work today as if second nature to her she could watch all the happenings going on down the road while she knitted away to her heart's content.

"Did you read it…the sign…did you see what's on it?" Agnes was doing her best to read it from the inside of the window.

"I'll check it at lunchtime…if we don't hear about it by then." June hung her coat behind her chair she had a lot of work to do with pension day tomorrow.

Not happy to wait, Agnes put her knitting aside and when Mr Oakley had turned his back she was out of the door to read the sign.

"…it says 'No Credit'…wonder what that's about?" Agnes was only in her chair when Mr Oakley appeared from behind the paper stand.

"If I may interrupt your work for a moment ladies?…well those of you who are actually working!" He gave Agnes a look that would turn cream sour.

It seems he'd had a lady in the post office early in the morning he'd only opened up and she was in the door behind him with two small children looking for milk and bread and she would pay him later on in the week when her husband brought home his wages. She'd practically begged him said she had nothing to give the children for their breakfast.

"I want none of that carry on around here…do you understand…this is not a charitable organisation." He huffed his way into the back room and left them with their mouths open.

That poor woman June thought to herself the humiliation alone of having to ask and then to be refused. How could he even do that he really was a frosty nature of a man. She wished she had been there to serve her she would have paid for it herself to think people were that badly off that they had to put themselves at the mercy of the likes of Mr Oakley. It wasn't right she had goosebumps she couldn't get that woman out of her head.

Agnes was very quiet all morning come lunchtime June asked her if there was anything she wanted to be brought back June liked to go for a little stroll at lunchtime to get the circulation going again after sitting all morning.

Chapter 6

"I think I know that lady she was in here last week looking for credit too…told her she would have to talk to Mr Oakley…wish I had helped her out now I feel awful…he's so hard-hearted…should have known he wouldn't help…"

Agnes was truly put out about the whole thing June had never seen her like that she was always so cheerful not even old Oakley would get to her normally.

"Can you remember what she looked like? …maybe she'll come in again." June listened intently and she was convinced she had just described the lady and her two children who had recently moved into the house down the road from her.

But surely there were no money issues there the dad was always well dressed and the girls were always immaculate. She hadn't seen much of the oldest lad but the one time she did he didn't look like he was lacking in any way.

Walking home she thought *what if*? What if it had been her? What if only a couple of doors away a mother had nothing to put on the table for her children.

There was no sign of the children playing in the garden. Today wasn't a very nice day anyway. *They were probably playing indoors*, June thought.

Lighting the fire when she got in, she wondered if they were cold if maybe they couldn't afford to light a fire?

She would have to be more vigilant keep an eye out for them over the next few days.

While chatting to her mother on her next venture into town June talked to her about Mr Oakley and the sign he'd put on the window of the post office.

Valerie poured the milk into her tea as June spoke about her concerns about her new neighbours. Again, she noticed the shake in her hand it wasn't from the excitement this time.

"Be careful June…I mean…people have their pride…I know I've been there."

She went on to talk about her days of boozing and how she hadn't the price of a cup of coffee by Monday after getting her measly allowance while working for Joe's aunt. She'd had her room free so her wages were very little but she managed to buy cheap beer to feed her alcoholic needs.

Food was never first on her priority list when shopping she remembered taking the leftovers after dinner in the evenings and hiding them in her room until she would have the old woman put to bed. Then she would scoff the lot down with her beer. To this day she remembered the manky taste of the cold cabbage she could never bring herself to eat it since.

There was a lot of truth in what Valerie had said, June thought to herself as she sat on the bus home. The last thing she would want to do is to embarrass the woman but she would like to help her out.

The front door was open as she walked past not wanting to seem nosey, she looked straight ahead and as she passed the gate there was shouting.

Half afraid to look back she could hear a door bang and practically hopped before it closed on the latch.

Goodness, June thought it's going to be difficult to find a way to get close enough to offer help there if possible at all.

Looking around her kitchen she wondered what her Nan would have done probably be round there with a pot of chicken soup no questions asked just the neighbourly thing to do.

She would bake some biscuits and bring them round for the children.

Small steps!

She wasn't sure if it was Heidi or Sarah who had answered the door, they were very alike though one was older than the other. Closing the gate she turned to wave goodbye to see the mum, Maddie holding the plate standing at the door and smiled what looked like a smile of gratitude.

It was just a small gesture but maybe in time they might become friends.

Valerie wondered if it would be ok if maybe next time they meet up that they could meet up in Nan's house or rather June's house she promptly corrected herself. June was delighted that she wanted to call she would make dinner maybe do some cabbage! They both laughed.

It had been a while since she'd had company for dinner. She would do a roast, put it in early and do it slowly so that it would be nice and tender.

A glass of wine would go very well with this she thought as she cut the meat in thin slices almost falling apart it was so tender of course it wasn't an option not with Valerie coming to dinner.

"Aww...you shouldn't have they're beautiful...come in...come in." June took the beautiful bunch of flowers from Valerie and let her in past her in the hall.

As they sat down to eat there was a knock on the door it was Heidi from down the road returning the plate from the day before. This time June knew it was Heidi because Valerie was on her heels soon as she opened the door.

"What's your name? ...aren't you very good to bring the plate back to June?"

June was amazed to watch the interaction between her mother and the little girl.

"...let me see...I think I have a sweetie here in my bag...do you eat sweeties?" As Valerie went back to the kitchen to get her bag Heidi looked on with eyes wide open.

"...there you are and one for your sister too..." Valerie smiled at her and Heidi took the silver wrapped sweets in her hand.

"Thank you old lady." she was swiftly out the gate running and skipping down the road to her house before the door was closed.

"...don't know if I like being called an old lady." Valerie closed the clasp on her bag as she walked back to the kitchen laughing.

It was a beautiful bag red a with diamond-like clasp.

Valerie saw that June was looking at it and probably wondering how she could afford such an expensive-looking bag.

"...it was Joe's aunt's...he gave it to me when she died...rest her...do you want it? ...here I'd like you to have it."

She started to empty out all of her things out of the bag and that was when June saw the tablets they'd fallen on the floor.

"No not at all…I was just admiring it it's really nice…no you must keep it…Joe gave it to you after all…but thanks." She picked the tablets up off the floor and handed them to her mother who made no remark on them at all.

Agnes was late today, after ten and no sign of her.

Mr Oakley paced up and down looking out of the window each time he passed.

Coming through the door like a hurricane she gasped.

"I'm so sorry…I never sleep in…don't know what happened." With a look that would skin a calf Mr Oakley turned on his heel and was out of the front door at great speed content that Agnes was in and the place was in good hands. June wasn't at all sure that he trusted her never seemed happy to leave her on her own. Thinking back to when Mac had the post office she remembered being on her own a lot of the time, different times altogether.

Different people too like chalk and cheese!

"Was he giving out…I suppose he was…wretched old man…he's miserable."

June had to smile at Agnes.

"…put the kettle on…there's a good girl…I'm parched for a cup of tea…was up half the night with my old bunion…gave me grief alright…it's no wonder I had to drag myself out of the bed today." Yawning as she spoke Agnes looked as if she hadn't even washed her face there were creases on one side of her jaw where she must have been lying funny.

June put the kettle on and made her a nice cup of tea.

"Why don't you get that bunion looked after? ...I'm sure there's something you could get to relieve the pain." She handed Agnes the tea with a biscuit from the kitchen.

She had just filled the biscuit tin that morning herself, there was only ever a plain old biscuit in it so she thought she would treat them to some nice chocolate ones.

"...thank you dear...oh! ...no...I couldn't let anyone at my feet...no...I'd rather suffer on...aren't they funny things too...feet I mean..." Looking down at her bunion she enjoyed her cup of tea.

"...aw...that's better...you know Jane...when I was about your age I could dance all night...had twenty pairs of high-heeled shoes...loved my shoes...would spend all of my money on shoes...can hardly walk now never mind dance..."

As June went back to her own desk, she thought to herself, *My name is June...not Jane...*

The door of the post office opened and slammed shut the breeze had caught it.

"Oops! ...sorry." The customer hadn't expected it to close so fast and wasn't quick enough to catch it before it slammed.

Looking round June could see it was her new neighbour and recognising June she turned and went out again.

June followed her, at last she might have an opportunity to help out.

Holding Sarah her youngest by the hand she seemed embarrassed using the excuse that she'd forgotten her purse.

June invited her for a cup of tea in the cafe across the road it was about time for her morning tea break anyway it would be great to have a chat and get to know her better she thought.

"But I have no purse..." Maddie was apologetic but June soon convinced her that it would be her treat and that maybe

Sarah would like a glass of orange juice too. The cafe had a play area for children so it was the ideal place to have a chat Sarah could play away to her heart's content while still within view of her mother.

They talked for a while mostly small talk June wondered if she would ask her how things were financially or would that be rude.

As if reading her mind Maddie while watching Sarah closely broke into a full conversation of how hard things were how she was struggling to make ends meet after which she apologised for burdening June with her problems when they hardly even knew each other.

June assured her it was ok and that she would love to talk some more but that she had to get back to work she had already taken more time than she should not wanting to be rude while Maddie spoke so she promised to call in to June at home in the evening. June would make them something to eat and they could chat.

It had been blowing a gale all day and the post office door had all but blown off its hinges by evening June couldn't wait to get home she would go to the butchers on the way and get some nice lamb chops.

Cutting the turnip she thought of Nan there was a constant smell of turnip in the house back then Pop loved it. There'd be bacon ribs and turnip one day lamb chops and turnip another day and always on Sunday there'd be whatever meat Nan would cook and turnip.

It was a devil to cut though, Nan showed June how to wrap a clean tea towel on one end of the knife and use the handle on the other end so that you could bang it through the turnip. To this day it knocked the sweat out of her but it was worth it mashed with a bit of butter and a pinch of pepper sure you couldn't ask for more. Maddie didn't let her down she was at the door at eight o clock as planned and on her own. Sam the eldest was now old enough to be left with the girls and she wasn't far if they needed her. There was no mention of her husband and June didn't ask.

She didn't half enjoy the chops and mashed potatoes with turnip she had it devoured in minutes. At first the conversation revolved around the children Sam the eldest was a good boy looked out for his sisters and was a great help around the house. Heidi the middle child was a bit of a madam loved to dress up could see her walking up the street in her mother's high heels although a mile too big for her and Sarah the youngest was a daddy's girl through and through.

June wanted to ask about the dad but the conversation changed before he came into it. She would wait.

They'd been on the housing list since Sam was born living in a one-bedroom flat with three children before they'd been offered a house the rent was a struggle, compared to the rent in the flat it was a good bit more. It was great to have the extra bedrooms she said but she'd lie awake at night worrying about the rent if they'd fallen behind, they could lose the house and be out on the streets.

"Do you mind my asking what your husband does for a living?" June had waited long enough it was bugging her to find out. Maddie kind of shuffled uncomfortably in her chair going on to say that he did his best to support his family seemingly played music mostly busking on the street. Some days he would do well but the winter months were hard. Music was his passion he wasn't happy doing anything else.

It's no wonder June thought they're finding things hard that man needs to get a proper job and support his wife and family.

Talking to Valerie the next day when she stopped by, she was disgusted at the selfishness of the man.

"Passion…I'd give him passion I'm telling you…he'd be out of that door to work and earn a decent living…passion!" June thought this was true sometimes you have to put your own needs aside.

"…do you think he treats her ok?" Valerie seemed concerned her way of thinking was that he was the type of man that did what he wanted regardless of his responsibilities sounded to her like he was a bit of a control freak.

Out busking while his wife looked after the children at home on very little by the sounds of it and probably expected his pleasures on top of it all.

June told her mother to stop, that she was getting a bit too graphic for her liking.

"…didn't you meet him on the bus one day…how did he seem to you?" June thought back to that day he'd seemed ok she hadn't noticed him carrying any musical instrument though, maybe he wasn't busking that day.

Valerie took her tablets out of her bag and got up to get a glass of water June had noticed her hand shaking again.

"…it's a price I must pay for my misspent youth…" She'd noticed June watching her and went on to explain how the alcohol addiction had left its mark a small price to pay she said things could have been a lot worse, she was one of the lucky ones that had got out on time. She had put it all down to meeting Joe, he'd got her on the right track saved her from herself and the demon drink.

"...do you drink June?" June could never say that she was a drinker she would sip a glass of wine just to be sociable but that was as far as it went. She could take it or leave it. In fact she couldn't remember when she'd last had a drink. Probably would have been with Mac on one of their nights out with the wholesalers she'd had many a good night out on those occasions, Mac did enjoy the wine though often ending up using June as a crutch to walk home.

All good memories.

June asked her mother if she'd suffered any other health issues as a result of her drinking seemed she had trouble with her legs too had circulation problems. Wasn't sure if it was as a result of her drinking or smoking but had always put any of her complaints down to one or the other and of course there was the guilt she had carried all her life and probably would bring it to the grave with her.

Greta was in a state when June called by. She'd put down a bit of weed killer she'd found in the shed to try to control the weeds in the back garden careful not to put it anywhere near the chicken coup. It was getting impossible to get down to the line to hang out the clothes with the nettles and she'd swore the last time she'd got stung that she would do something about it. She was tidying the shed when she came across the container of weed killer it was ancient must have been there since the year of dot but what harm would it do, she would try it. Only as it turned out, it did cause harm. She found Mrs Sheridan cat stretched at the back door when she went out the back a few days later but then she thought it had been nearly a week since she'd put it down and it had begun to kill the nettles alright.

Surely it wouldn't have affected the cat at that late stage? But on reading the container she discovered it probably had. Now she had cursed that cat a million times but she would never harm it she was very upset.

June went with her to talk to Mrs Sheridan who though heartbroken to hear about Snowy was very understanding towards Greta who was visibly upset by the whole ordeal. After three cups of tea and Snowy's life story, they parted as friends.

Snowy was given a prime spot in Mrs Sheridan's front garden where all those years ago her husband had found her in the snow. She vowed never to get another cat it was too heart breaking to see them go. She would indeed miss her mischievousness and of course her company.

She never did keep her kittens.

Valerie had an appointment with the clinic she'd had an ulcer on her leg that kept her up all night with pain. It just didn't seem to be healing.

June offered to accompany her it was a lunchtime appointment and she would have her lunch on the way, Valerie was so glad of the company it was a cold old place in the clinic. June had been there years ago for a dental visit while in school she remembered having a tooth pulled and walking home with a white cotton pad sticking out of her mouth. Soaked in blood by the time she'd got home she still remembered being afraid to take it out in case she would bleed to death.

The nurse at the clinic was very cold and sharp and Valerie appeared to be petrified though only going to have her leg dressed.

Going home on the bus June thought her mother appeared to be dragging the leg when they got back to her flat, she sat down straight away and rubbed it.

"It's so sore…probably the new dressing…" There were tears in her eyes.

June thought to herself, *this wasn't right,* she got a chair and lifted her mother's leg up on it and she gasped. "…no…it's too sore for that love."

The sweat was rolling down her face, June knew she couldn't leave her in that state though she was already running late for work.

"Will I maybe loosen the bandage do you think?" She felt for her mother she was in such pain.

As she nodded to do so June undid the bandage to find that the felt like dressing was sticking right into the wound and it was all inflamed. She wanted to take her mother back to the clinic straight away but she told her that she wouldn't be able for it and asked if she could do anything with it.

Nervously she got a tweezers from the first aid box and scalded it with a kettle of water, she made three attempts to prize the corner of the dressing out of the wound before she finally got it. Valerie was gripping her jumper with the pain.

This was cruel, June thought no one should have to suffer like this.

"I'm so sorry I'm late back…will make up for it." June walked right into Mr Oakley on her return literally bumped into him at the door. He'd been checking the window display Agnes said. She couldn't get her mother out of her head she hoped that by now she might have had some relief it was so careless to leave the dressing like that surely more care should have been taken to assure the comfort of it. It was sore enough without adding to it. She would call over to her later maybe ask her to stay with her for the weekend to rest it she'd mentioned Joe was going to have to stay over for a few days on his next job.

He wasn't too happy about it but he had to go where the job took him and he wasn't often asked to go out of town in fairness.

As she walked past the new neighbours there was shouting, the window was open and she could clearly hear the row going on as she passed the front door opened just as she got to her own gate and the dad appeared rushing towards their gate followed by Maddie who was sobbing, "Why won't you love me?"

June didn't know where to look, should she go back to her! Maybe not she wasn't sure what to do. Turning the key in her door she appreciated the quiet of the house sometimes the quiet could be daunting too but today after the day she'd had with worry about her mother and now after hearing the goings-on down the road she was grateful for the peace and quiet.

Chapter 7

She sat at the table feeling totally drained turning to reach for the post she'd left there after picking it up in the morning she froze for a moment. She could feel someone standing behind her she'd left the front door open in her eagerness to sit down.

"Heidi…goodness you gave me a fright…are you ok…have you been crying?"

She'd seen June passing and followed her home her mum was crying and she was afraid.

"Daddy is gone…" June reassured her that everything would be ok and that they would walk together back down to her house in case her mum would worry.

Maddie was smoking in the kitchen she'd told June in their last conversation that Dan used to keep her in cigarettes. He would bring her a pack every day after busking.

"Maddie…are you ok?" June told Heidi to go and play upstairs and she would look after her mum. She'd stuck the cigarette into her arm and was crying with the pain.

On asking about the other children she told her that Sam had taken Sarah and Heidi to the swings Heidi had come back for her coat in the middle of a blazing row.

"I saw her run off…knew she would be safe with you…I think he's gone this time June…he'd gone a hundred times before…but this time he told me he didn't love me anymore…I love him so much…so I do…I love him so much, why doesn't he love me? I don't know why…" She was a pitiful sight.

June took the cigarette and told her that harming herself wouldn't sort anything and that she had the children to think of. Whether he had gone for good or he'd be back again like a hundred times before as she said to herself she was going to have to look after herself, her self-esteem was at a very low ebb.

June tidied up around and Maddie seemed to settle she thanked June for her help and promised not to burn herself again. June had seen the marks before and thought it may have been her husband, she had been so wrong.

She wondered why she would want to stay with a man that didn't love her would she not be better off on her own at least have some self-respect and not be treated like a doormat as she so obviously was a convenience to look after his children and satisfy his needs.

As she got up to go Dan came up the garden path he looked enquiringly at June as they met halfway down the path, she wanted to face him tell him to appreciate what he had but she felt almost intimidated by him she said nothing.

She would close the door behind her this time she didn't like the look on Dan's face she didn't trust him he actually scared her. As she walked down the hallway to the kitchen the doorbell rang. Half afraid to open it in case it was him she watched from the window and waited until the person walked back down to the gate to see who it was. It was Valerie she knocked on the window and called her back. The leg had eased a bit so she decided to get a bit of exercise the flat was quiet without Joe around. June told her of the drama down the road and Valerie advised her to stay clear.

"Give that crowd a wide berth…I'm telling you…they'll be thick as thieves again and you'll get caught in the middle of it all…you'll get no thanks for it."

She knew her mother was right she would have to stay out of their affairs after all they had survived before they had moved in beside her that was that she had her own worries to cope with.

Valerie was delighted to stay for the few days while Joe was away turned out they got on very well. They seemed to have the same interests liked the same foods except for cabbage! Valerie June discovered was really fun to have around sore leg and all. She would have the dinner ready and the kitchen tidied when June got in from work the few days went by so fast and they promised to do it again. June actually missed her when she left the house was so quiet without her laughter she had such a hearty laugh she almost envied Joe having her around.

Greta had called round for tea a couple of times while she was staying and as they reminisced about their younger days June could see that they had been very good friends growing up.

"Would you like to live to be really old?" Valerie was sitting back in Pop's old chair with her sore leg on a stool looking very much at home.

Greta laughed. "Sure we're not far off now…an old man said to me once…" Greta looked thoughtful as she went on.

"The secret to old age is a hot water bottle."

Valerie was in stitches laughing.

Wiping the tears from her face she inquired as to why a hot water bottle would have any relevance to reaching old age.

Greta went on unapologetically. "It may burn...but it won't nag." And on that note, she bid them goodnight and was off down the road laughing to herself.

June quietly wished things could stay that way forever it felt so right her mother being there but then there was Joe.

"Did you see that?" Agnes was all but in a state of shock as Mr Oakley walked away from her. June hadn't seen what went on but she knew it would all be revealed within minutes Agnes wasn't one to keep a secret.

He'd actually given her a compliment along with a bar of chocolate said it was great to have somebody to rely on to keep things ticking over in his absence on days he had to be somewhere else.

"...I don't think he's well...wonder what's in the chocolate." Agnes was so funny.

"Maybe he really appreciates your efforts...isn't it nice to be appreciated?" June had found it a bit strange herself totally out of character of the man she'd come to know but then she thought he might have another side to his character too.

"...maybe...maybe he likes you! ...might be taking you for a stroll in the park next...if you play your cards right." They both laughed.

"...what and me with my bunions...and him with his bockety knees...we'd make a nice pair alright." Agnes took off one of her shoes and rubbed her bunion.

"...I'll be keeping an eye on you two." June really enjoyed her company.

She wondered if she had any family there was never any mention of children or a husband or anything about her home life come to think of it June thought.

Only just her bunions she talked quite a bit about her bunions.

Mr Oakley came out of his office and walking past Agnes on his way out he smiled at her.

"…he's definitely not himself today." Agnes reverted her eyes very quickly.

"I'm a bit worried about Joe." Valerie was waiting outside when June finished work. Delighted to see her they walked back to Nan's together.

Seems Joe hadn't been the same since his return from working away.

Not wanting to interfere June chose her words carefully in reply as to why her mother had felt that way about him, Valerie told her he'd not been sleeping very well was walking the floors half the night and when she'd asked if anything was worrying him, he'd snapped at her. Which wasn't like him at all.

June tried to put her mind at rest and said it would probably blow over maybe he was just tired, *he worked very hard and he wasn't getting any younger,* June thought to herself. She hated to see her mother so worried-looking she would leave the pile of ironing she had promised to do and they could call round to Greta for an hour she would cheer her up.

Unfortunately they'd called on the wrong day the usually cheerful Greta had been to visit a friend in the nursing home in town and she was down in the dumps in very low spirits afterwards.

"It's such a sad existence…I know they're well cared for and all that but…it's so very lonely for them…surely when someone isn't well isn't it better that they have their family around…oh! I don't know." Greta went on to talk about her visit well into the second cup of tea. She'd met an elderly man on the corridor as she went to get a vase of water to put her flowers in for her friend and he'd taken her by the hand and asked her where he was.

There were tears in her eyes he'd said his family would be looking for him they wouldn't know where to find him.

"…I hope I will have my independence to the day that I die…sure who have I to look after me either…probably end up down the same road…maybe that's what's so upsetting." She wiped her eyes with the end of her apron and apologised for burning their ears with her tales of woe.

Valerie seemed to have lost the worried look from her face as she listened to her friend while being supportive as ever in her listening.

June assured Greta and indeed Valerie that she would always be there for them even though age didn't come into it both twice her age but that didn't mean anything she could be gone before them.

"How about we get the bus into town and treat ourselves to a nice coffee and a big cream bun?" June hoped her suggestion would lighten the moment it was all getting a bit too morbid.

Nobody had control over the future and worrying about it wasn't going to change anything that's what she always thought anyway. Greta was up the stairs to put on her glad rags and Valerie was smiling again. Turned out to be a lovely evening had a few laughs a nice cup of coffee and the biggest bun on sale in the shop.

Valerie got off at her stop just down the road from her flat and June and Greta waved her off as the bus continued on its journey to their stop.

Walking Greta to her gate June mentioned how Valerie was a bit worried about Joe and how the trip into town had seemed to cheer her up.

Greta agreed too that it was indeed very out of character for Joe to be acting like that and wondered why and hoped everything was ok with him.

Valerie got home to find Joe in a state she pleaded with him to talk to her and after a great deal of persuasion it all finally came out.

She'd known he'd been abused as a child or interfered with as his aunt had put it. He'd only ever mentioned it once to her and she could see it had been painful to him to remember so she never went there again. But she wasn't aware that he wasn't the only one. There had been two of them both ten to twelve years old camping in the summer holidays.

It was only yards from where they lived but it was to be a great adventure. Joe stopped talking and took a shaky breath.

His expression became hard and angry.

The poor man, Valerie thought, this torment had stayed with him all of his life and more than likely had robbed him of his childhood years.

But what had happened while he was away to stir it all up again?

They had been sent to a building site to cover holidays along with half a dozen other labourers from other sites. Their boss ran a big company had sites all over the place and employed dozens of men. At first, he didn't recognize him but while on tea break, he had come up to him.

"Thought it was you…" When the man standing in front of him took off his hat, he recognized him straight away.

"Bob Bob…" Both men had embraced they'd been friends all through their school days many years ago now. They hadn't much time to catch up then but arranged to meet for a drink after they'd finished.

Bob Bob, named so because of his stammer at school which only developed after that horrible night, *no longer seemed to stammer must have outgrown it,* Joe thought to himself but the name had stuck.

He'd been living only a few miles from Joe and Valerie's flat after returning from working on the buildings abroad.

Joe couldn't believe they hadn't met in all of those years and they were only a few miles away from each other. Valerie listened tirelessly as he went on and on about how they reminisced about the past. Suddenly his face changed, Bob Bob had brought up that dreaded unforgettable night that they had gone camping.

A memory he'd said that had been the cause of his marriage breaking up had played so much on his mind that he couldn't bear for his wife to get close to him. He'd turned to drink and drank every penny he'd earned while working abroad and he'd worked so very hard for every penny. It had ruined his life, so much so that he only now so many years later had felt strong enough to face his abuser.

He wanted Joe to go forward with his story as well he would organise for him to speak with the right people and they would go about it the right way.

For all they knew that man was still terrorising young boys.

Joe wasn't at all sure he wanted any part of it he'd put it behind him after years of misery and didn't want it haunting him again.

Whether that be right or wrong he wasn't sure and that was what was tearing him apart and he was very sorry to have taken it out on Valerie.

Valerie would be of no help in his decision as far as she could see the past was best left in the past but then Bob Bob did have a point. What if that man had abused others? What if it was still going on and some other innocent child was carrying that memory as well that torment that robs you of everything?

Was Joe strong enough to go through with it though?

She wasn't sure looking at the state of him in only talking to his friend about it she wasn't at all sure.

They would meet again and maybe discuss it further Joe seemed more relaxed after unloading what was on his mind. Valerie watched him as he went to wash his face wet with tears and bearing the scars of a life of carrying a heavy load around with him. He looked much older than his years and especially today. He dragged his feet as if exhausted he hadn't been sleeping.

June was shocked to hear her mother's story as they chatted over dinner the next day in one way relieved that she didn't seem worried about him like before. Well she was worried but at least now she knew what she was worrying about.

Her mother had told her that Joe had been interfered with but no more was ever said. She felt for him and she offered any help she could give, Valerie looking at her sincere face told her not to fret. She was sure that if Joe did decide to go down that road and she really doubted that he would there would be professional people able to guide them through it. It could be a long road and there would be plenty of bumps along the way she reckoned that's if he did decide to take that route. Bob Bob would be taking action regardless he'd said he wouldn't be pushing him but he hoped he would make the right decision.

June wanted to ask more about this man but didn't want to seem nosey.

How were they going to contact him for instance it had been over fifty years she reckoned a lot of water under the bridge. *He could be dead,* she thought to herself.

Valerie was thoughtful for a moment then she suddenly started to cry.

Joe had confided in her years ago but now she wanted to shout it out for all the world to know to shame him into apologising to those boys, now older men for taking away so much from them and for scarring them for life.

"It was Bob Bob's uncle…he was home on holidays and had brought him a tent as a present…helped them to put it up in a field nearby…and then…well let's just say…he'd had his wicked way with them." Valerie blew her nose and excused herself.

She went on to say that at such a young age they were naive and vulnerable, believed him when he told them it was a normal thing to do but they weren't to tell anyone especially not their mothers and fathers.

The boys had kept it to themselves for a while but it all came out when Joe, thought to be suffering from grief after his mum and dad had split up only to lose her to drink and his dad to far away fields was sent to counselling by his aunt after spilling it out emotionally, she'd noticed his anxieties a long time before his mum and dad had split up.

The signs must have been evident it didn't take long for the counsellor to diagnose the problem. Joe too afraid of the consequences had said it was a stranger that he'd never seen him before which was true in a way but there was no mention of Bob Bob or his uncle.

Of course the counsellor had said that there was a lot of grief in relation to the loss of his mother at such a young age as well and his dad not to be seen for dust.

Joe was placed in the care of his aunt who he stayed with until he came of age and moved out then when he got work as a labourer. Got his own place but continued to visit his aunt almost every day.

June was sitting with her mouth open.

"His uncle? …goodness!" She was gobsmacked.

Valerie got up to go and asked her to keep it to herself, it wouldn't do for it to get out now not when Bob Bob was on the verge of taking action.

His uncle it seemed had since moved house but had become somewhat of a recluse hadn't been seen around out only to stock up on supplies on the rare occasion Bob Bob had said.

He was still alive living somewhere outside of town. Bob Bob hadn't said.

"…how he can live with himself I'll never know…" Valerie was livid.

She thanked June for lending her a sympathetic ear and was on her way.

Those windows won't be cleaned today, She thought to herself.

She'd had great plans to clean the windows and change the curtains earlier in the day but not now she was all over the place.

Agnes looked lovely when she came through the door of the post office the next morning smiling from ear to ear.

"Don't you look well…going somewhere nice after work?"

June thanked the customer in front of her as she put her pension into her purse.

"I'm going out for lunch actually." Agnes was using her grandest accent looking all posh and walking with a swing in her hips, *no sign of any bunion pain today,* June thought to herself with her wearing high heels. She'll be nursing her bunions for the week she had to smile to herself.

"…anyone we know? …or maybe I shouldn't ask." Sitting with her elbows resting on her desk she admired this hard to put an age on lady and was delighted to see her going out for lunch.

As she spoke Mr Oakley appeared in the doorway, she hoped he hadn't heard the conversation he would be coming to the conclusion that they hadn't enough work to be doing and too much time on their hands to be chatting.

He was actually smiling not particularly in the direction of June more towards Agnes's direction.

"…I see…" June whispered across to her work companion only to be shushed promptly. Mr Oakley had appeared from behind the counter and was all ears!

"I will be taking Agnes on a business lunch this lunchtime…" clearing his throat he continued, "…would you mind very much taking a later lunch…I would be much obliged." June agreed and assured her boss it would be no trouble at all.

As he disappeared into his office, she looked across to Agnes who was now wearing only one high heel and rubbing her bunion.

"…business lunch indeed…you'll be crippled in those heels!"

Agnes agreed and regretted wearing them although they did look glamorous and gave her a bit of height she had said seeing as she was only knee high to a grasshopper and shrinking every day. She would suffer them.

Chapter 8

Valerie was going to make something special for tea garlic potatoes butternut squash and chicken. It was Joe's favourite she might even stretch to a nice desert although she was counting the pennies at this stage. She was finding it even harder to make ends meet these days the work wasn't coming in and the bills were never ending.

Joe could hardly wait to tell Valerie his news Bob Bob had told him how he'd traced his uncle seems he'd had his mail delivered to a friend's house in town when he moved house, he had to have an address to redirect his mail and his friend was delighted to oblige. Bob Bob had said if he only knew the man, he wouldn't have remained a friend not to mind being so obliging. He would pick it up on a regular basis when he would be in town to pick up his pension. Had worked for years in the insurance business abroad and came out with a nice pension and moved home.

Valerie wondered how he had come across this information Joe too had wondered but Bob Bob assured him it was from a reliable source. Not revealing anything just a slight tilt of the head and a wink.

"I don't know, Joe…sounds a bit fishy to me." Valerie wasn't at all comfortable with this.

Joe put her mind at rest straight away he had given it a lot of thought and had come to a decision.

He had struggled through his teenage years had serious thoughts of doom and gloom in his darkest hours when he'd felt there was no way out of the torment in his mind, he'd even considered taking his own life.

For some reason or other he could never actually see himself doing that.

He was done with it he wasn't going to put himself through it again that man had done enough damage. Going forward with a complaint against him as was what Bob Bob intended to do would mean seeing him again and he never wanted to lay eyes on him again. He'd wished him luck with his proceedings but told Bob Bob he'd put that part of his life behind him and he hoped his uncle would be brought to justice he really did, maybe this was a coward's way of doing things but he'd made his decision. He wouldn't be pursuing it any further.

Bob Bob promised to keep in touch and assured him that his uncle would pay and pay dearly for his abusive behaviour if it took the rest of his days and every penny he owned to bring him to justice he would.

Whether it be the right or wrong decision Valerie wasn't sure but she could see the relief in Joe's face and that was enough for her tonight they would have a nice dinner and relax it had been rough few days.

June had picked up a few scones in the bakery shop on her way home and was going to call in on Greta but as she approached her gate Greta was coming out of the house. All spruced up and looking lovely.

June greeted her with a smile not mentioning the fact that she was on her way to have a cup of tea with her and a nice scone.

"I'm off into town to meet Valerie…might stop at the bakery and pick up something nice for her." June handed her the scones and told her it would save her a trip not wanting to take them June insisted and told her to enjoy them.

She watched as she ran to the bus stop she would have missed the bus if she went to the bakery, she thought to herself.

As Pop used to say, "T'is an ill wind that doesn't do someone good."

Agnes had been quiet since her business lunch with Mr Oakley and June didn't like to ask, she would tell her if there was anything to tell.

There wasn't a word out of her only her head down working away which wasn't at all like her maybe a nice cup of tea she thought.

Mr Oakley wasn't to be seen either not that she was complaining he was such a miserable character.

"Nice cup of tea Agnes?" June handed her the cup and a couple of chocolate biscuits.

They chatted for a while but there was no mention of the lunch or Mr Oakley.

She wasn't herself though June decided to ask her if everything was ok.

She didn't know an awful lot about Agnes only that she was really good company she was kind and caring and they had become good friends.

"I am in agony the last couple of days Jane…I could cry with the pain…those wretched shoes nearly killed me…I'm not joking with you…I'm in agony." Agnes rubbed her leg.

"…thank goodness…I thought something had happened on your lunch date…or rather your business lunch, wasn't it?" They both had a giggle.

Mr Oakley it seemed was ever the gentleman treated her so kindly and hoped they might do it again sometime. Only next time she said she wouldn't be wearing heels they were gone in the bin.

June thought she would never have put those two together not in a million years but then they say opposites attract!

Wasn't it nice at their age she wasn't sure of either of their ages but she reckoned they were both fairly well into the Autumn of their lives, *never too late,* she thought to herself there's hope yet!

She thought of Matt and how the years had gone by regardless of her feelings.

"Time and tide wait for no man," Walter would say that. She could still see him tipping his hat as he'd go on his way dear Walter.

The basin was brought in for a week after that and the bunions were pampered daily with no remarks from Mr Oakley only a sheepish look as he passed by Agnes at her desk and a clearing of his throat as he passed by June.

Valerie had enjoyed the scones Greta had said when June called by for a chat and a cup of tea, she thought she had looked well and was in good form June was glad to hear it. She hadn't been talking to her for a few days not since the business with Joe. She wondered if her mother had told Greta about the goings on but there was no mention of it. She would call on Valerie in the next day or two having given her and Joe some space.

She had hoped Valerie might call on her.

Passing Tilly's she decided she would go in and give her mother a ring she could wait until she got home but it would be too late then to arrange something.

She would never use the phone in the post office it was too risky she didn't reckon that Mr Oakley was so infatuated at the moment that he wouldn't notice.

"I have something to tell you." Valerie wasn't saying much she would call to Nan's in the evening and all would be revealed. June was puzzled, *it must be something to do with Joe and Bob Bob,* she thought and continued on her way back to work.

The afternoon had dragged on and June was glad to see the door of the post office close for the day. As she passed by her new neighbour's house on her way home Heidi the middle child came running out of the gate not looking where she was going, she'd run straight into June. Her brother came running after her.

"No...no." She hid behind June as she passed shouting at the top of her voice.

"Whatever's the matter?" June stopped for a minute.

"Give me back my pencil." Sam rallied her round June and Heidi had practically pulled the skirt off her before she was finished.

June opened her bag and took a pen out of it and handed it to Heidi.

"now give your brother his pencil back." Heidi took the pen and handed the pencil to Sam.

It was only a pencil bitten and chipped why would they fight over it, June thought to herself. She followed them into the door and knocked to say hello.

Sam immediately blocked her view saying that his mother was out.

"No she's not...she's here." Heidi was peeping out from behind him. He pushed her away from the door and stood facing June boldly. He was a big lad very much like his dad June wasn't about to argue with him.

She could tell by the smell of cigarette smoke that his mother was indeed in the house but for some reason or other he didn't want June to know.

"Is everything ok Sam? You know if I can do anything...you only have to ask." June was concerned.

"...we don't need anybody's charity...thank you very much." He slammed the door his mother must have been asleep and the bang woke her. June was just closing the gate when she came to the door looking like she'd just got out of bed a half-smoked cigarette in her hand. The ash fell to the ground as she squinted her eyes with the light.

"June...come in...come in." June didn't feel at all comfortable about going inside.

"...I'm sorry about that...must have dozed off in the chair." She looked frail even more frail than she looked last time June had seen her it had been a while. She was evidentially still self-harming by the marks in her arms, *it was such a sad existence,* June thought. The house was cold and unwelcoming there was no offer of tea. The floor looked like it hadn't been swept the table bore an oilcloth covered with tea stains and there was a small hill of ashes coming from beneath the grate in the fireplace speckled with cigarette buts.

Sam had disappeared up the stairs and Heidi sat with her feet curled up under her on the chair. There was no sign of the youngest child Sarah, June thought, *she must be out with her dad no sign of him either.*

She had promised her mother not to get involved with this family but how could she not they were crying out for help she would do what she could.

"…Maddie…what can I do to help…Maddie?" June wasn't sure what it looked like to be depressed but this woman was out of it and it wasn't a drink there was no sign of any drinking going on. It looked like she'd given up on life and on her children, she was like a lost soul.

"…why is mummy so sad?" Heidi twirled her hair round her fingers beautiful auburn curls neglected not having been washed and her clothes much the same.

Suddenly Sarah appeared from behind the door sucking her thumb also looking neglected.

"…where is your dad?" June asked Heidi only to get a shrug of her shoulders.

Sam thumped his way down the stairs and out the front door she watched as he passed by without a look or seemingly a care for his sisters.

June put her bag on the table and wondered where to start she made a cup of tea for Maddie scalding the cup first. It smelled like she had had an accident in her pants there was a smell of urine as she leaned over to give her the tea.

"Would it be ok if I help you to tidy up a bit…do you think?" June wasn't sure if she would bite her head off or give her the go-ahead or maybe not answer at all.

"…Dan…my Dan…he's gone June…he's gone this time for sure." Her face bore no expression she was just staring across the room. Was she drugged? Surely not, not with young children in the house!

Something wasn't right though June was sure of it.

She felt for the children who seemed accustomed to the filth and dreariness of the place.

There was no hot water so she filled the kettle as many times as it took to get the children clean and the kitchen as well, she dare not go upstairs she didn't want to imagine what that would be like. She got Heidi to get a change of clothes for her sister and herself and put the dirty ones in a bag to take home with her to wash.

All cleaned up they looked so pretty Heidi got quite excited and brought some ribbons for her hair to June asking her to put them in her hair handing her sister a few as well.

There was no place for tears June told herself though her heart was breaking.

She hadn't noticed their mother watching.

"…thank you June…I'm such a waste of space…it's true for Dan." Maddie got up and stumbled onto the floor her voice sounded a bit mumbled.

As she lifted her up June could feel her bones. "…how long is it since you've eaten? you are so thin…you need to mind yourself." June wanted to give her a good talking to but now wasn't the time she would ring her own doctor she didn't like the look of her.

The girls started to cry and June assured them that their mother would be fine she was just a bit under the weather and the doctor would look after her.

Dr Mc Cabe didn't waste a minute he took one look at Maddie and carried her into his car to the hospital Heidi was hysterical as Sarah just looked on.

There was no way of knowing where Sam had got to and no sign of Dan, June didn't know what to do she couldn't leave them on their own. She waited and waited looking out of the window hoping someone would come. She decided to take the girls up the road to her own house and at least she could feed them, there was nothing to speak of in the cupboards there. She left a note to say she'd taken the girls to her house.

As they dug into some leftover cottage pie that June had reheated for them which was supposed to save her cooking for dinner she kept a watch out of the window. It was getting dark when there was a knock on the door.

"Mummy…Mummy." Heidi ran to the door. It was Sam looking very concerned.

After explaining what happened to him June's heart went out to him, he'd seen his dad busking earlier in town he would go and get him he bit his nails as he spoke his hands filthy.

She offered him a bit to eat before he took off but he said he wasn't hungry.

Both girls hanging out of him he assured them he would find their dad and so he did leaving his gear on the street he raced home to his girls with tears in his eyes and white as a sheet he enquired as to what had happened and how it had come about that the girls were with June.

Sam had just told him to hurry that there was something wrong with their mum.

She sat him down and made him a cup of tea which he drank with one of his girls on each knee Sam was very quiet.

"Sam will look after the girls now and I will go and see about your mum."

Dan thanked June and promised to let her know how Maddie was on his return.

He didn't seem quite as scary as she thought more vulnerable in fact. She wondered what had gone wrong they must have loved each other at some stage.

Was it money or the lack of it that had caused trouble in paradise?

With all the goings on June had completely forgotten about Valerie she was to call over in the evening she would never think to look for her down the road in Maddie's house. She would give her a call in the morning she was exhausted now.

Would Dan call after the hospital or would he wait until morning? She wasn't sure she would stretch out on the sofa in case he called. Poor Maddie she hoped she would be ok.

Awoken by the daylight June had pains and aches everywhere after spending the night curled up on the sofa and she felt cold. Dan hadn't called. *Maybe it was too late,* she thought probably didn't want to call so late.

A quick shower and off to work she hadn't realised the time she was running late.

The post office was hectic for some reason or other and Mr Oakley was like a demon Agnes didn't seem in great form either she would keep her head down and get on with her work.

Leaving a gust of wind in his wake Mr Oakley went off once things had died down Agnes was huffing and puffing.

"The cheek of some people…who did he think he was dealing with." June looked over at her work companion half afraid to ask.

"...put his hand on my knee...he did...cheeky as you like...I put him in his place I'll tell ya...taking liberties and we only walking out...huh!" June smiled to herself Agnes was all red and flustered.

"Cup of tea, Agnes? ...got some nice chocolate biscuits yesterday..." June got up to make the tea but Agnes was still giving out.

"...taking liberties...I'll give him liberties...huh!"

Sounded like the romance was over before it even started!

Dan was looking out for her as she walked past on the way home.

"Oh! ...how's Maddie?"

He bowed his head as he told her it had been too late she'd taken some painkillers lots of painkillers. June was in shock she knew she was a bit out of it and she did have her suspicions regarding drugs but only for a split second she couldn't see a mother do a thing like that while looking after her children so she'd put that thought out of her head as quickly as it had entered it.

Dan asked her inside the children were upset and he wanted to be near them. As she sat down Heidi came over to her and cried into her lap Sarah was sitting with Sam and the place looked nice and warm and tidy. The grate had been cleared of the ashes and there was a nice fire on. Just a few simple improvements that made such a difference.

June apologised to Dan for not realising that Maddie was in trouble and said that she wished she had called the doctor sooner Dan assuring her in his reply that it wouldn't have made any difference told her he had appreciated what she had done and there was no question of her not getting the doctor on time.

He only wished he could stop blaming himself for the whole sorry situation. They'd been having problems for a long time not to speak ill of the dead but he said that Maddie was very possessive of him he couldn't be late home or she would say he was cheating on her or even keep down a job since she'd embarrassed him in his last one.

He'd had a good job in a factory had a car on the road and all, things were good but her jealousy led her to convince herself that he was having an affair with a girl he worked with when he was only obliging her with a lift home in the evenings.

She was waiting for them outside work one day and had called him all sorts in front of his workmates the embarrassment was such that he could never bring himself to go back there.

He'd turned to drink for a while lost his confidence and self-respect along with any feelings he'd had for Maddie she'd driven him to it with her possessiveness and jealousy and what could only be called mental abuse.

Of late he'd only been there for the children she would shout and threaten to overdose but he never thought she would. He'd left for good the previous day just couldn't take the mental abuse any longer no matter what he did it always came back to his uselessness she'd told him he was good for nothing.

"Comes a time when you can't take anymore," he'd said.

He put his head in his hands and cried aloud Sarah ran to him and Heidi followed with Sam to follow shortly after her, arms around each other huddled in a little corner.

If only Maddie could have seen past her possessiveness and jealousy it was obvious this man loved her he was a broken man, a pitiful sight.

The memory of that moment huddled together in their grief would stay with June for the rest of her days.

Left on his own now to rear his children the busking had to take a back seat.

He would struggle on his small pension allowance but he would do his best for his children and promised to keep their mother's memory alive.

They'd had good times too he wasn't going to forget them. June would be there for him if he ever needed help with the children or indeed just someone to talk to.

Sam had become mature overnight had apologised to June about the day he'd closed the door in her face.

"I was ashamed…ashamed of my mother…" He broke down as he spoke.

"…am I the worst son…" June hugged him until he had cried enough.

Chapter 9

Valerie was in tears as she listened to June's story.

"That poor man…and those poor kiddies…" She talked of how she had hit rock bottom herself at one time in her life. It was the drink of course but she'd been one of the lucky ones she'd come out the other side with the help of Joe.

"…which reminds me…" Her face had changed from a look of hopelessness in talking about the family down the road to a look of elation in talking about Joe.

June remembered she had said she had something to tell her she was still thinking about her mother hitting rock bottom and was finding it hard to shift her attention to what her mother seemed to be bursting to tell her.

"…Joe has asked me to marry him…" She was waiting for June's response and mistakenly thought she wasn't happy about the news. Her face dropped.

"Sorry Valerie…what did you say…" June couldn't get the image out of her mind of her mother with nobody around to help her when she had been through so much, she apparently didn't know half of it.

She hugged her so tight that Valerie gasped and both ended up laughing.

"I'm so happy for you mam…" Without even thinking June had called her mam for the first time since they'd met. *She didn't even seem to notice,* Valerie thought, it just seemed to be automatic it was a warm feeling she'd never felt before. She made no remark.

They talked for hours the wedding would be in June Valerie wondered if June might be her maid of honour.

"…have to give up those cream buns." June tapped her tummy and they laughed. This was the best news she'd heard in a long time and boy did she need good news she'd been so troubled and unsettled since Maddie died and those children's cries had gone through her. For a moment she had felt happy again and she was happy for Valerie very happy indeed.

Though Agnes had never met her mother she'd hugged June and congratulated her on the good news.

"Oh! I do love a wedding always makes me cry…" And she was off to the ladies' room blubbering away.

As she came back to her desk Mr Oakley came in the shop door.

"I'm so sorry Agnes…I didn't mean to upset you…I am so ashamed." He took his handkerchief from his trouser pocket and offered it to her.

June looked on thinking this was very cavalier of him, he'd always struck her as a country gentleman although moody she always thought there was another side to him and she wondered what had happened in his life to make him so, well cranky with people.

He cleared his throat in passing June as usual she thought and went into the back of the shop to his office.

Out of sight and earshot June asked Agnes what she had said in reply to the offer of his handkerchief she wasn't sure if anything at all was said but she would ask anyway.

"…sure what could I say…he thought I was still upset over his hand on my leg…on the business lunch last week…you know…remember how upset I was and indeed still am…but not the sort of upset I'd be crying about…no…more like…well let's just say…more like vexed…he vexed me…but sure I took it anyway…was a nice gesture…albeit the wrong reason." Agnes wiped her nose. "…wonder does he want it back?" She laughed holding the handkerchief in the air.

"I'll give it a wash and return it tomorrow…he is a kind sort really…a bit cheeky but kind." June had a real big soft spot for Agnes she certainly had a mischievous side to her there was no doubt about that.

Handkerchief washed and neatly pressed she returned it to Mr Oakley they were on speaking terms again and he wondered if he might make it up to her by taking her for lunch another day perhaps.

He would be out of town on business the next day so they would meet up for lunch the following day.

Agnes looked very pleased with herself there wasn't much work done the next day only the bit done in between fitting on skirts.

She'd brought five skirts into work with her to ask June's opinion.

"Do you think this one is a bit tight…although I do like the colour?"

"..do you think this one rides up a bit when I sit down?"

"...what do you think of this one? I made it myself...it's beautiful tweed."

"Oh! I don't know Jane...I think I look fat in this one...do I?"

"...jeepers...I'm worn out...what do you think of this one?"

Having fitted on all five skirts while June tried to keep up with her customers Agnes sat down with sweat rolling down her face.

"...we're slaves to fashion...aren't we?"

June chose the skirt she had made herself it was the best fit and looked really nice.

"You can tell him you made it yourself when he admires it...and he surely will."

"...you're too kind...but yes I think I will wear that one...best put them away or they'll be thinking we're getting into drapery around here." She bundled the skirts into a bag and sat contently behind her desk. Job done.

"...did you know Jane I worked in haberdashery when I started working first...yes...I spent five years working there...I know every size needle and every colour thread on the market...I loved it...closed down...gave us loads of thread and needles and stuff when we were going...never be stuck still have most of it." June wished she would call her June and not Jane!

Mr Oakley came into work the next day looking down at the floor a very brief 'Good morning' and into his office. Agnes looked at June inquiringly and June shook her head he certainly didn't look his usual self.

When he came out into the shop an hour later Agnes made a loud sigh.

"Mr O...what?"

His face was covered in a pinkish rash turned out it was some kind of allergy.

"...Only allergy I have is to cat hair...don't know of anything else." He went on his way looking like a scalded cat not to mind an allergy.

"...goodness..." June jumped in her seat as Agnes shouted out.

"...the handkerchief...I washed the cat's blanket in the same water...wasn't dirty just rinsed it out to freshen it up...no point wasting clean water..." She was red in the face.

Would she tell him? How could she? The poor man she would get him some calamine lotion it would calm it for him that's what she would do.

It would be of no advantage telling him that she was the cause of his rash no advantage at all maybe down the road a bit if, well if things developed at all.

Maybe they would have a laugh about it then!

Walking home June had to laugh to herself when she thought of Agnes. She'd asked Valerie round for dinner and thought it might be nice to ask Greta as well for the chat.

There was a knock on the door and Valerie got up to answer it. June was taking a roast out of the oven and just about to leave it on the table.

Looking down the hallway thinking Greta was a bit late she was surprised to see Dan from down the road at the door. It had been weeks now since Maddie had passed away and she hadn't seen that much of him or the children. She'd often dropped in a few scones in the passing of an afternoon when she would take a notion and bake or in meeting them on the street, she would offer to help out in any way but he'd never taken her up on the offer. *He seemed to be keeping them very close never let them out of his sight it must be so hard,* she'd thought.

"Hi, Dan…come on in…" She called him into the kitchen.

"I'm so sorry to call at such an awkward time…I can see you're about to sit down to dinner…maybe I will call another time?"

"…not at all…come in…sit yourself down…haven't seen you for a while." She pulled a chair out from under the table but he continued that he wouldn't be staying long. Sam was watching the girls and he didn't want to leave them too long.

He'd taken an offer from the council of a house swap in a different area it was too difficult to continue living where his wife had passed away. The children were having nightmares and he couldn't leave them for a moment.

They needed a fresh start somewhere where there weren't any bad memories where the children weren't haunted by the past.

June would be sorry to see them go she was just getting to know them and the children were so lovely.

They would be moving out at the end of the week and he just wanted to tell her himself and not have her find out from hearsay.

She had been a good neighbour and he knew his late wife had begun to trust in her too. He appreciated all the help she had given them during that awful time when he'd lost his wife, they would remember her for her kindness to them.

He handed her a small box of sweets but it may just have been a box of gold coins it meant so much to her. They had nothing, yet however small the token he wanted to show his appreciation June felt a bit sad she'd only known them for a short while. She didn't even like the look of Dan when she'd seen him first he used to scare her but as it turned out he was a lovely man mentally abused over the years by his wife. Jealous and self-harming she'd made his life hell in the latter years.

Valerie sat in the background listening to the conversation she'd felt so sorry for Dan on hearing what went on she was a bit concerned about Greta who was never late especially when there was dinner involved.

As June closed the door after waving Dan off, she just caught a glimpse of Greta huffing and puffing her way up the garden path.

"I'm late…stop…I was leaving the bin outside to save me doing it later…you know…I don't like having to go outside in the backyard in the dark…" She shrugged her shoulders and continued.

"I get the creeps in the dark…spiders and all that…anyway didn't the darn wheel come off the trolley…it's just a little hand trolley my poor husband made to take the weight of the bin…sure there was I wondering why it was so heavy…stop."

Walking into the kitchen she plonked herself down on the nearest chair.

Wasn't long before she and Valerie were deep in conversation June continued with serving dinner and left them to it.

The gravy had gone all lumpy it was so long simmering away so she made a fresh pot she loved gravy.

She remembered Nan used to say, "You could have a pair of old socks on the plate there…long as they were covered with gravy you'd be digging in…"

Nan had taught her to make the best meat gravy ever she didn't often have visitors for dinner but they would always comment on her gravy.

Valerie had gone on to talk about Joe and the wedding probably be a small affair Joe would more than likely invite some of the old neighbours from where his aunt lived. He'd got to know some of them pretty well over the years and they were still keeping in touch.

Greta of course would be invited and if June wanted to ask her boss and that lady that worked with her Valerie couldn't remember her name so June enlightened her. "Agnes."

"...Yes...do ask Agnes to come too...now let me see..."

As she racked her brain to summon up all of her friends June could see she was struggling there weren't many.
June cleared the table and thought to herself, *A nice piece of apple pie for desert...that should do nicely.*

The evening had gone well and having put all but the world and its master to rights they parted in good form Greta would walk Valerie to the bus stop and June was to put her feet up after waiting on them all evening.

She would leave the cleaning up until morning she was exhausted lying awake for what seemed like an age she thought about Dan and the children.

One would think, she thought to herself, *that having been married with three children and now having a home for themselves that they would have been nicely settled for life one never knows she agreed with herself and finally got to sleep.*

"June...June." Greta was waiting to see her pass by on her way to work next day.

"Morning Greta...you ok?" June had come without her umbrella and was debating as to whether she would go back for it when she heard Great call her.

"...have you heard from Valerie this morning?" Greta looked concerned.

June replied that she wouldn't normally hear from her that early in the day and wondered why Greta had asked.

Greta assured her that she didn't want to worry her but that she herself was a bit concerned about how Valerie had stumbled on her way to the bus stop for no reason apparently no bump in the road or anything she could trip over she had just stumbled.

She wouldn't hear of Greta going with her on the bus though she only wanted to ensure her safety in getting on and off so she wondered if maybe June had heard anything. "...I'm sure she's fine..." She waved June off to work as she agreed with her that Valerie was probably fine though she was a bit concerned. She would call on her after work.

The counter was busy all morning seemed to be a lot of new faces in too along with the regulars. Not even time for a cup of tea poor Agnes was flabbergasted by lunchtime.

As the door closed for lunch the kettle was promptly put on the boil.

"Not even a decent biscuit in this establishment after all our hard work..." Agnes seemed very disappointed. June offered to go to the bakery around the corner and get a couple of nice cream cakes they deserved a treat.

Walking quickly around the corner getting soaked in the process she thought of Valerie she hoped she was ok, not wanting to make a fuss she would casually call round after work for a cup of tea maybe she would pick up a nice cake now as well while she was at the bakery. It wouldn't be unusual after all for her to call round she often did in fact, there wouldn't be a week go by without her or her mother calling round to each other. They had become good friends.

There was a smile on Agnes's face again, *nothing like a cream bun to cheer someone up,* June thought as she picked up her cup to tidy up before Mr Oakley came back.

Seems Agnes and him were having their business lunches as they called them on a regular basis of late. Not in a million years would she have put those two together, but then she thought they say opposites attract.

Valerie answered the door looking very pale and tired she hadn't slept very well she'd said.

"Hope it wasn't my cooking." June tried to make light of the moment but she was a bit concerned about her at the same time.

She told her to sit back down where she was and she would make her a nice cup of tea and a slice of coffee cake just freshly baked in the morning.

Valerie smiled as she watched June make her way around her kitchen only a small kitchen but served its purpose they weren't the fussy type were happy with what they had.

"Joe was saying Bob Bob was in touch…he's meeting him for a chat this evening after work…" taking the cup from June she thanked her for the lovely cake.

"…what ever happened to Bob Bob's parents…only there was never any mention of them…was there?" June pulled out a chair from under the table and sat down holding her cup between her two hands she liked to do that it could be so warm and comforting.

Valerie put her cup on the table and took a run to the toilet returning looking even paler than she was.

"…are you ok…you look so white?"

"…I'll be fine…some sort of bug or something I picked up I'd say…" Sipping her tea she started to get the colour back into her cheeks and proceeded to tell June about Bob Bob's parents. Joe had spoken about them often a lovely couple spoiled Bob Bob rotten him being an only child and some had said they had been very lucky to have him they were that bit older when they married.

Bob Bob had done very well in school and won a scholarship to further his education, money wasn't a problem seemingly so he would have gone far either way. But he'd had brains to burn Joe remembered Bob Bob's dad saying it would do him good to go away to college make a man of him. He would say he'd give all he had to see him smile. In all of his achievements and there were many he'd always seem a bit sombre, a bit distant.

Joe remembered feeling the very same way it's hard he'd said to hide something so awful inside and look happy on the outside. Valerie remembered he'd cried as he said that.

As it happened Bob Bob's parents passed away in a car accident shortly after he went off to college, the car had skidded on ice and they ended up in a ditch. Found the following day both had been killed on impact. That was the end of college for Bob Bob he'd never returned started to do odd jobs around the place and whatever he could get on the buildings, such a waste Valerie said.

His uncle had a lot to account for he'd not only taken his childhood and Joe's as well and goodness knows how many more, but he'd ruined any chance he'd had in life to make anything of himself.

In the end he sold up and took off Joe hadn't laid eyes on him until they'd met recently on a job.

"…I don't want to pry but…do you think Joe will pursue things further…I mean with Bob Bob?" June hoped she wasn't being forward in asking.

"…no…I don't think so…he hasn't discussed it in a while…I don't think so though…it's probably a very hard thing to do…to go back there…even in thought!"

Walking home, June thought, *how horrible it must have been for those two young boys and to crown it the man was someone they had trusted not that it would have been any better had it been a stranger but someone they trusted!*

Greta was standing at the gate as she passed by and invited her in, Valerie had given her the rest of the coffee cake to take home as she didn't trust her stomach with having any more of it nice and all as it was.

After chatting for an hour and finishing off the coffee cake between them Greta walked her to the gate happy to hear that Valerie was ok and it was only a bug.

"Well aren't we devils for worrying…wouldn't be happy if we're not worrying about something sure…thanks June…it's a load off my mind…sure we're killing one another half the times…but if anything was to happen to her…I don't know what I'd do…good night love…" June waved to her as she turned the corner, she too was relieved to see Valerie. She would call on her again in a couple of days just to make sure she was ok.

Walking past Walter's old house, vacant again she wondered who the new neighbours might be, the next occupants. She hoped she would come to know them too over time.

Joe was bursting with news as he came through the door Valerie was upstairs when he shouted up to see if she was home. He'd met with Bob Bob for a drink after work. He'd brought him up to date with the recent happenings regarding the event of their childhood.

Bob Bob had tracked down his uncle and had called on him only to be shocked by his appearance when he opened the door.

Chapter 10

Still holding on to the memory of a big strong build of a man overpowering him as a child Bob Bob had said that he was nearly sick as he walked up the passageway. Instead there stood before him a frail old man grey in both his face and his receding hairline.

Not recognising him he inquired as to what his business was and quite sharply asked how he knew his name.

He'd just turned and walked away it was visibly apparent that life had punished him enough, his hiding away from the world his frail appearance and the bitterness in his voice was proof that his guilt had weighed heavily as a burden through the years.

Bob Bob had said there would be no going forward with a complaint for him at least now he might be able to put it behind him there was nothing to be gained for either party in raking up the past. Joe had said he was relieved and that he had no intention of going forward with the complaint anyway he was glad Bob Bob had found peace with himself at last.

Valerie was relieved too she knew Joe so well and she knew he would be forever wondering if he'd done the right thing in leaving it all in the past having had the opportunity to bring it out in the open and not taking it.

They could now move on and plan their wedding she'd secretly looked in a few dress shops she wouldn't be wearing a white dress she thought she'd gone past that. She would wear a nice costume maybe and a lace blouse just to have a bit of lace. She almost feared getting too excited in case anything would go wrong she always felt weary if things were going right good things just didn't happen to her.

She would ask June to meet her in town after work, time was moving on and even if she had picked out a costume it may need alterations. She was handy with the sewing machine herself but she wouldn't chance it this time she'd probably make a mess of it with the nerves and all.

June was delighted to go shopping with her mother but they both agreed it may be better to go at the weekend and have the whole day meeting up after work wouldn't give them much time for the shops and lunchtime would give them less.

"June…I have written down my vows…would you like to look at them…see if they're…you know…ok?" Valerie took a piece of paper out of her purse and handed it to June. Looking at it had put her in mind of the piece of paper she had handed to her all that time ago now with her phone number on it.

Back then she had no intention of ever ringing that number now here she was getting to know her mother a bit more every day and realising how much she had missed down through the years. She thought of Matt.

They'd just come into the café for a break from the shops. Legs walked off them and still no costume to suit they had carried a cup of tea and a sit-down.

June hesitated as she opened the piece of paper.

"Should I? …I mean are they not private? …between you and Joe?" June wasn't sure she should be the first to hear them.

"…I want you to…go on…please?"

It was just a couple of lines very short but beautiful.

"…Joe…I never want to be so far away from you that I can't hear your heartbeat…

"I promise you however far we go in life…when you look back…I will always be there…

"…I love you."

"…that's beautiful…beautiful…" June gave her mother a hug and in her heart, she knew she had meant every word. She was so happy for her she so deserved a bit of happiness.

She still had a vacancy in her own life she wondered if ever she would fill it.

She wondered if she would ever love again.

Back to the shopping again June's feet were beginning to give in why didn't she wear a comfortable pair of shoes they must have walked miles in and out of every shop.

Then as they passed a second-hand shop, they both gasped as they saw it on the window not a costume but a very elegant cream lace dress with long sleeves and a high collar on the neck, trimmed with lace also. It looked perfect.

Agreeing to just have a look at it they went inside never having bought anything in a second-hand shop they were a bit worried. As they asked the girl to take the dress from the window to have a look at it an old lady passed them by.

"That would be perfect on you dear." Valerie looked around but she was just going out of the door, well-dressed she put her in mind of Joe's aunt. Hair in a bun at the back of her head and very neatly dressed.

There were questions going around in her head as she looked at this beautiful dress being sold for a song would it have belonged to someone she knew maybe and they might recognise it on her on the day? Or perhaps someone had died wearing it. She wasn't at all sure but it was beautiful.

Returning to see how they were getting on the assistant agreed it was indeed a beautiful dress and that it had only been put up on the window five minutes before they came in the door. It had been left in by an elderly lady just a short time ago she'd said. "You could have seen her going out as you came in."

June looked at Valerie was it that lady that had said it would be perfect on her? She had to at least fit it on June said just to see how it looked.

It could have been made for her there would be no alterations needed it was a perfect fit.

Walking down the road Valerie was very pleased with herself she was amazed at how well she looked in the dress and assumed it would have been expensive to buy in a shop. It had a lovely feel off it and sort of rustled when she walked.

It smelled fresh like cotton she did very well to get it so cheap as well.

Valerie insisted on treating June to lunch they'd not eaten since their eleven's and had walked around the shops for at least two hours had certainly worked up an appetite.

Sitting by the window June noticed the lady sitting across from them.

"Isn't that the old lady from the second-hand shop? …the one that had left in the dress?"

Valerie looked up from her lunch menu and looking over her reading glasses she agreed.

She wanted to go over and talk to her thank her for the lovely dress that would now be her wedding dress. She didn't want to intrude though she was a stranger and *she would probably embarrass her,* Valerie thought.

They had pancakes with maple syrup for lunch and chatted for nearly an hour.

"Oh! …hello…did you fit on the dress?" The old lady from the second-hand shop was standing by Valerie when she looked up from her pancakes.

Delighted to have the opportunity to speak to her Valerie invited her to sit and join them for a minute.

Taking the bag from under the table she gave her a peep to see she had indeed bought the dress and bought it for a song.

Her name was Alice, as she introduced herself she went on to tell them that the dress belonged to her mother long since passed on she'd never had the opportunity to wear it herself.

She'd often taken it down from the closet she'd said and just looked at it going on to say that her mother had looked beautiful that day. The wedding photograph had taken pride of place on her mantle for as long as she could remember.

"…I do hope it will bring you the happiness it brought her." She fondled the dress delicately.

She had been an only child her parents as much in love after their forty years of marriage as the day they'd wed. The dress was wrapped in black tissue paper just as it had come in the box hadn't faded at all she remarked.

Valerie told her it was to be her wedding dress in June and she thanked her for her generosity in parting with it, it was clear it meant a lot to her in the way that she almost caressed it in her hand.

She smiled and told them it brought her great joy to think that it would be worn again it was far too beautiful and exquisite to be left in a box.

They parted and Valerie couldn't help but feel a tinge of sadness as the old lady seemed to well up as she wished her luck on the day, she wondered what her story was. She was truly a lady and in looking at the beautiful dress in her bag Valerie thought, a very well-to-do lady too.

June had it at the back of her mind to ask Valerie if she would like to have Nan's wedding ring it seemed the right thing to do and the perfect time. Had she been around it would have been given to her and not to June when Nan passed.

She wondered though if maybe Joe had bought a ring already and didn't want to upset the applecart so to speak. *It wouldn't do any harm to ask*, she thought to herself, she didn't have to use it on her wedding day but she thought it would be nice for her to have it.

As if reading her mind Valerie looked at her watch remembering she had arranged with Joe to meet up after the dress shopping to go and look at some rings.

"Won't be anything expensive…we're not into that kind of stuff anyway even if we could afford it…" She smiled at June. "Just a token on the day."

This was her opportunity why didn't she bring it with her up to now she had only thought about giving it to her but now she knew she would.

Valerie was ecstatic when June mentioned it, she cried and squeezed June's hand so tight it took the colour out of it.

"…you know June…to be honest…I was going to ask about my mother's ring…even before the wedding was arranged…I just wondered if maybe she was wearing it when she died and it was buried with her…I have nothing of hers…" She sobbed into her handkerchief and June was so pleased she had offered it to her before she had asked. Why hadn't she thought of it before it was rightfully hers after all.

There was plenty of bits and pieces that she could have had, June hadn't thrown anything out they were safely stored in Nan and Pop's old bedroom. Tidied away as if an end of an era. She knew someday she would have to part with them but somehow she never had been ready. She would ask Valerie round to go through them and let her take anything she wanted there was nothing of value as such just to those who loved them.

As they opened the big old suitcase a feather flew out of it both looking at each other smiled. "Don't think we're on our own." June picked it up and put it beneath a statue of St Jude her Nan's righthand man she would pray to him every night without fail before she turned the light out.

"…my goodness…" Valerie kneeling on the floor in front of the suitcase held a plastic-covered item of clothing in her hands it looked very small.

"…it's your christening dress June…and it was mine before that…she'd kept it all those years…" Opening it she shed a tear and held it to her heart.

June thought she would never stop crying she cried for all the years she'd lost in her growing up she'd cried for her father and she cried for her mother whom she'd lost many years before she'd passed at all.

It was time for a cup of tea a strong sweet cup of tea, June thought.

"…thanks June…I mean…for this…for letting me come here and…you know." Valerie was off again June thought to herself maybe it will do her good to have a good cry she had many years of heartache built up inside.

As she watched her mother touch the christening gown affectionately she wondered, *what she could be thinking then,* she had a thought.

"What would you think of making a ring cushion? …maybe…just…well at least it would be putting it to some use…and along with it we'll be including a nice memory…maybe…it's lovely material?" June wasn't sure it was a good idea after all Valerie seemed to be miles away.

"…sorry June…yes…yes that would be lovely…that would be lovely…"

The christening dress was made into a beautiful satin ring cushion filled with the remnants not to mention a thousand memories to puff it up. It would bring one very happy moment from the past into the present for Valerie she'd said as she sat admiring it when she attached the last stitch.

The post office would be closed for two days to have necessary work carried out as Mr Oakley put the notice in the window Mrs Kelly came through the door.

"Two days…what will we do for the milk and the bread?"

Totally ignoring her little rant Mr Oakley pushed his glasses up on his nose and cleared his throat while disappearing into the back office. Agnes in an effort to cover up his rudeness assured Mrs Kelly in her softest voice that she could stock up the day before and that the work wasn't happening for a week or so giving people plenty of notice so that they could be prepared. The nearest shop to buy milk in was a good distance away but there was the bakery around the corner for the bread.

"…sure we couldn't afford to be buying in the bakery…them with their fancy packaging…three prices on everything…fancy names on the bread…sure isn't it all flour at the end of the day…" Mrs Kelly wasn't at all impressed.

June got her bits together and put on her coat the evenings were still chilly no sign of the spring yet although the daffodils had begun to show in Nan's garden. She couldn't yet call it anything but Nan's garden though a few years gone now she still thought of it as Nan's.

Bidding Agnes a good afternoon she wondered why she hadn't begun to put her coat on as well she seemed to be in no hurry at all. She was only around the corner when it started to rain and she'd left her umbrella in a bucket under her desk. She would go back and get it more than likely she would need it in the morning anyway. The door was still open but Agnes wasn't at her desk as she took her umbrella from under her own desk, Mr Oakley came from the back of the shop followed closely by Agnes.

June was so embarrassed they hadn't seen her and were chatting away and being very intimate with each other. She didn't know where to look Mr Oakley was sitting on Agnes's chair now and Agnes had him pinned down while taking his glasses off. She would make a noise to let them know she was there she couldn't be listening to their intimate conversation it wasn't right.

She opened the drawer in her desk and slammed it shut.

Taking her umbrella and scarlet in the face, she bid them goodnight. Mr Oakley had lost his balance and slid off the chair Agnes cool as a cucumber waved her off and turning to Mr Oakley she said:

"There now Mr O…it was a little hair that was in your eye…lucky I was blessed with good sight…yes…and a steady hand." She winked at June as she closed the door behind her.

June had obviously felt more embarrassed than Agnes but she wasn't sure how she was going to face Mr Oakley in the morning!

Greta was all in a tizzy when she came to June's door only in from work June had plonked herself down on the nearest chair seeing Agnes and Mr Oakley together was just about all she could take for one day.

"Oh, June…I think I've put my foot in it…" She'd met Fr Mulcahy and happened to mention Valerie and Joe getting married. He was highly offended that he hadn't heard about it himself it would usually be the norm for the priest to be informed before all in sundry he'd spurted out he wasn't very pleased at all.

But why? I mean Valerie is no longer living in the parish why would he be upset…maybe? June had a thought.

Valerie had discussed having an informal affair for her nuptials a registry office but she hadn't discussed it for a while. She thought to herself, *What if she could be married in the local church? Would that be something she might have considered.* She would ask her and wouldn't it be nice after all it was where she had been christened made her Holy Communion and her Confirmation.

Valerie had already considered it but seemingly thought with her past record and all sure the old biddies in the community would have a field day.

No, she thought, *it's better to steer away from all of that,* although she would have loved to have had a proper church wedding.

June wouldn't comment though she herself wouldn't have let a bit of gossip interfere with such an important day in her life. That was all in the past now and most of the old biddies as Valerie had called them had passed on.

However it was Valerie's day and as long as she was happy that was all that would count.

"Morning…" Agnes was first into work next morning usually the last to show her face she gave June a start when she opened the door.

Bursting to talk about the evening before she followed her over to her desk.

June reassured her it was absolutely none of her business and only for the umbrella she would not be any the wiser, what went on between Mr Oakley and her was of no interest to her at all.

"…we have been stepping out now for a while…you know…he's very shy though…well not with me of course……but…you know what I mean." She winked at June and went back to her own desk.

June would like to have said they were well matched and she was happy for them but two more different people you would struggle to find. She couldn't see how they would ever get together.

The wedding was only weeks away. Valerie and June would spend every weekend together tying up loose ends changing plans inviting and uninviting the list had changed so many times but the final figure had to be given in to the venue within the next few days.

The invitations had been handmade Valerie was very knacky with making things every card was made to suit the person to whom the invitation was going. Be it a dear friend or a lovely neighbour or someone who served her in the local coffee shop all personally written and crafted to perfection. There was no doubt Valerie had a gift in design a wasted talent.

"June…there was something I have been meaning to ask…" June listened intently to her mother while sticking a stamp to she hoped the last few invitations. Every day Valerie seemed to be adding a few more names to the list.

"You know how the night before the wedding…well the bride isn't supposed to see the groom." She didn't have to say anymore.

"Of course, you can stay…would be nice to go from Nan's…don't you think?"

Valerie started to cry, "I don't know if I'm doing the right thing at all…sometimes I…" She got up from the table and went upstairs. June waited for a few minutes but she didn't return.

As she climbed the stairs she listened for her and as she got to the top, she could hear her sobbing as she knocked on the bedroom door.

Opening it slowly she asked if it was ok to go inside Valerie apologised and told her to come and sit on the bed beside her.

She talked about Joe and how good he was to her but she wasn't sure that she loved him, was kindness the same as love? Would it be enough to keep them happy in a marriage?

June reassured her that every bride had their doubts as the big day got closer not that she'd had any experience in the matter but she'd heard it can be a very uncertain time.

"…what about your lovely words in your vows? …did you not mean them?" June got a smile back on her face. They hugged and Valerie agreed she was probably just doubting herself the nerves were kicking in. She hadn't wanted any fuss or even a hen night.

"I'm way too old for that kind of going on." She'd shrugged her shoulders when June suggested it but Greta had organised a little get together in her house for the week before the wedding.

Chapter 11

Just a few from the area invited June had asked Clodagh but hadn't had a reply yet. She hoped she would make it she would love her to be there Valerie had told her to be sure to ask her to the wedding so she had slipped a note in with the invitation card about the get together the week before. Anyone would think it was Greta that was getting married she was so excited, she had it planned right down to the ivory napkins that would have to be the same colour as her dress. June had described it as best she could not wanting to give too much away just the colour to keep Greta happy at her end.

As she left Valerie to freshen up June came down the stairs to the kitchen, Joe had come in without them hearing him and he was reading his newspaper contently by the fire. He was such a lovely man no fuss at all about his big day his suit was organised and he was happy to leave the rest to Valerie.

It had been months ago he'd said she was the one with good taste she'd chosen him after all June remembered when he'd said that. Valerie had been standing at the kitchen sink at the time and he'd given her a kiss on the cheek.

"Just let me know what everything costs…I have it covered." He'd winked at June and gone out to leave the women to what they do best.

Valerie had told her he even paid for her dress and hoped she hadn't chosen that one because it didn't cost much.

"Looking forward to the big day? …won't feel it now." June pulled out a chair and sat at the table opposite where Joe was reading his paper. She sat the opposite side to where she had been sitting while sticking stamps for the invitations she thought she'd better and not disturb things. Valerie was so organised little piles of cards to be posted other little piles to be handed to the locals and some yet to be written.

Joe looked over his glasses and smiled, if only he'd known how upset Valerie had been how she had doubted herself and her feelings for him.

If June had any doubt as to whether they were well suited or not she wouldn't have reassured her mother that it was probably nerves and that every bride has some kind of doubts but she was sure as she could be that they were well suited. Joe got up and went to the cupboard taking out a small box and as he walked towards June he looked out into the stairway.

"Hope she doesn't come down for a minute." He opened the box to show June the beautiful sparkly ring inside explaining that he knew Valerie was over the moon about having her mother's wedding ring for her wedding but he wanted to buy her something as well. It was an eternity ring and it was so beautiful.

"…do you think she'll like it?" His eyes alight with joy he went on to say that Valerie meant the world to him he confessed that he wasn't the most romantic of souls but that he would never let her down. He'd appreciated how she'd put up with him he wasn't perfect he'd said and his past tended to haunt him sometimes but Valerie always stood by him.

"I'd walk away from me sometimes if I could…" Quickly closing the box as he heard Valerie's footsteps on the stairs he winked at June and went back to reading his paper.

Just as surprised as June was to see Joe sitting there Valerie hoped he hadn't heard the commotion upstairs she'd felt much better after her little cry. Everything was just building up inside and needed to be released funny how suddenly everything can just seem right.

"Cup of tea?" Not the type to be all over each other a nod was enough to tell that they were happy to see each other. June would leave them to it and be on her way maybe call on Greta on the way home to see how she was doing with her plans.

"Come in…come in…don't bang the door a girl…I have the cake in the oven it will flop." Greta didn't have to tell June she'd been baking apart from the lovely smell when you came up the garden path she had flour on her face.

She excitedly took a box from a shelf above the sink she'd rooted out her old photographs and was making a collage to give to Valerie on the night of the get-together she'd used old wallpaper for backing and had an old glass frame that would fit in nicely she'd said. There was so much work put into it and so much love June thought what a lovely friend she was. Valerie would love it she told Greta and thanked her.

"…not a word now…you hear…I'm dying to see her face…sure this will keep us in chat for the night…so many memories…"

Mr Oakley seemed to be walking a bit crooked, June thought as he walked by her desk keeping her head down, she wondered if he might comment on the awkward moment in the shop a couple of days before but there was no comment. Not even a "Good morning". *He was an odd sort alright,* June thought to herself. He was only gone into his office and Agnes was on his heels.

Within two minutes she was out into the shop again looking fierce cross. June kept her eyes on her work she didn't want to get involved obviously things weren't too rosy in the garden today she'd thought.

"Men!" Agnes was furious she took her bag from her desk and threw it beneath it June looked away she dare not be caught looking. If Agnes and Mr Oakley had one thing in common it was their temper one as bad as the other.

There was a letter on the floor in the hall when June got home, she didn't have to open it to know it was from Clodagh she'd know her writing anywhere.

She would be delighted to attend the wedding she wouldn't make Greta's get together sadly but she was looking forward to meeting her mother and Joe. She'd said it had been too long since she'd had a catch up with June as well so she might stay a couple of days after the wedding if that was ok.

June was delighted she would reply to her straight away and let her know she would be more than welcome to stay with her for a couple of days, she could get to chat with Valerie as well as she would be staying with June the night before the wedding. It would be perfect.

Reading further on Clodagh went on to say that she was sorry that she would not make the get-together the week before as much as she would like to see Greta and all the locals but she was sure she would probably see some of them at the wedding. June was getting more excited as the wedding date got closer. Valerie seemed very calm June would call on her after work for a dress rehearsal. Honoured to be her maid of honour while Joe had asked a workmate of his to be his best man. Vincent had worked with Joe for years and Joe had been his best man a few years before when he married his childhood sweetheart Gabi. They had two children Teddy aged three and baby Blossom aged just ten months. They were delighted when Valerie had asked if Teddy might be her ring boy on the day. It would have to be rehearsed of course but they were sure he would be fine. Having had her last fitting of her dress June was excited to fit it on, Valerie had bought the dress a few years before and never wore it, June had suggested altering it for her as they were about the same size and exactly the same height.

Valerie looked a picture in her dress as they both stood in front of the mirror June thought her peach-coloured dress made Valerie's cream dress stand out even more the colour was a good choice and Valerie had made a great job of altering it, it fitted perfectly.

Both stuck for words they just hugged each other tightly for a moment and cried and laughed agreeing they both scrubbed up well.

Valerie had made a special tea and June smiled as she served up her potato cakes. Nan's specialty she would make them for tea every Friday without fail.

Valerie had said she would make them for tea every Friday as well when she was little and even up to the day she left. It brought her back and June too had felt a bit sad.

It's funny how something as simple as a potato cake could bring you back.

"...June...I called to see Fr Mulcahy...he has agreed to marry us in the chapel..."

"But..." June was delighted but she thought Valerie didn't want a church wedding?

"...I know...I said I didn't want it this way...but...well we were talking the other night and...well...it's sorted now anyway..." She was very pleased with herself and so was June.

There would be a rehearsal in the church on the eve of the wedding June hadn't had time to get nervous but she could feel the nerves beginning to kick in now with only a week to go!

Greta was all organised the table was set with lovely food and the cake looked beautiful in the middle of the table on a lovely glass cake stand just for show on the night she'd said it wouldn't be cut until the wedding day it might bring bad luck! She'd made a pink sash for Valerie to wear that had the word 'Bride' embroidered on it in black thread. June had organised the drinks just to help out just a bottle of sherry and a bowl of punch.

The locals started to gather all in their Sunday best Valerie was invited to dinner with Greta and June as far as she was concerned. She got such a fright when she saw all the people that she had to sit down. Greta fussed about the place with beads of sweat rolling down her face she couldn't do enough. Valerie was overwhelmed when she saw the collage that Greta had done for her, she just looked at it for ages and as she looked up to Greta who was standing nearby with tears in her eyes Valerie too had welled up.

They hugged for a moment and then it was back to the frame that held such memories for them both. They would go on all night talking about the different photographs and between the laughter and the tears it was evident that their friendship was one of affection, fondness, respect, loyalty, empathy, and lots of fun. No money could buy that kind of friendship and June thought to herself, *no man or woman would ever come between those two.* Some ties could never be broken.

"My sincere apologies for causing any awkwardness here in the recent past." Mr Oakley had come to stand in front of June shortly after she'd got in to work. At first, she thought she was in for a telling off though she was only a few minutes late. She'd called into Greta on route to thank her for the night before and got talking she promised she would call in after work to help to tidy up to which Greta answered "Not at all dear…sure it'll be done…if anything wait let the work wait."

June was sure she had heard that saying somewhere before but couldn't remember where or when.

She felt a bit embarrassed and didn't know what to say to her boss in reply so she didn't say anything he'd disappeared into his office as quickly as he'd appeared leaving her with her mouth open. There was no warmth in his apology it was merely a statement. Agnes was busy trying to look busy with her ear cocked she hadn't a clear view across the shop but she had seen him approach June's desk. He had barely closed the door of his office when she was over.

"Well…what did old Mr O have to say? …misery guts…oh!…he does vex me." Agnes plonked herself on June's desk obviously the romance had run its course or was it a case of 'true love never runs smooth', June wasn't sure but as she told Agnes her guess was as good as June's he'd just made a statement and turned on his heel and walked away.

If looks could kill poor Mr O as Agnes called him would be shooting up the daisies she was furious with him. Seems he'd got into a terrible twist that day after falling off Agnes's chair and blamed her that they had been seen and shamed in an office environment.

"It was disgusting behaviour he'd said." Agnes was all a fluster as she spoke.

"…be a long time before he gets another cuddle from me I'm telling you…huh!… who does he think he is!" Although she was angry with him June could see there was a bit of affection there for him too. The anger would pass hopefully things would calm down a bit before the weekend they were both invited to the wedding!

Greta had everything sorted when June called by on the way home not as much as a spoon to be washed up.

"You were busy…why didn't you wait and I would have helped…" June stood by the sink as Greta automatically put the kettle on.

Chatting as she went Greta was always so glad when you called by June thought. Leaving a plate of chocolate biscuits on the table in front of her and a pot of tea Greta went to the back of the kitchen door and took down an outfit covered with plastic like it had just come from the cleaners.

"What do you think?" Holding the outfit up to her having taken off the plastic that covered it Greta seemed very pleased with herself. It was a beautiful red costume looked like wool June thought trimmed with a golden thread and golden buttons on the pockets. It wasn't new Greta had said but she had only worn it once. "…would I get away with it…do you think?" Looking at the costume herself she brushed it gently with one hand while holding it with the other. June told her it was beautiful and asked her to fit it on.

She didn't have to ask a second time Greta was up the stairs with the greatest of enthusiasm. Going by her mother and them having grown up together June assumed they would be about the same age but Greta looked a lot older maybe it was because she didn't seem to take any interest in her appearance she couldn't ever remember seeing her dressed up. Her grey hair always neatly in a bun at the back of her head. As she came into the kitchen wearing the red costume and her hair tucked up under a cream hat June had to gasp you could be looking at a woman twenty years younger than the one that left the kitchen ten minutes before.

"Greta...you look beautiful...it's perfect...really...just perfect." June got up to fix the collar of the jacket that was standing up on one side. "...really lovely."

Greta smiled and thanked June for her opinion going on to say that when one lives alone at times like this someone else's opinion was nice.

"...wouldn't be fussy normally...you know...pottering around the house...sometimes I don't even look in the mirror...sure who'd be looking at me? ...but I really want to look nice for Valerie's wedding...you know..." She looked so sincere June felt a bit sad. She lived on her own herself but never really gave it much thought never really wanted anyone else's opinion as regards dress. This was a big day for Greta and June would make sure she would have the best day ever goodness she thought this is so sad!

Clodagh would be arriving the next morning and June spent the whole evening sorting out the spare room it had been a while since the bed had been slept in so she would fill a hot water bottle and put it in it to air it a bit. It would be lovely to see her friend again and lovely too to have a bit of company in the house.

Looking prim as ever Clodagh came up the passage to the front door, she had a bag and a box. The bag didn't seem too heavy but when June took the box to help her it weighed an absolute ton.

"It's a gift for Valerie and Joe…" Clodagh laughed as she hugged her friend.

"Come in…it's been too long…I'll leave this here…unless you want to take it upstairs?" June leaving the box on the kitchen table hoped she wouldn't have to carry it upstairs. Clodagh left her bag down and opened the box it was a lovely lamp looked like bronze and certainly weighed as though it were the real thing. The shade was an off-white colour and the base looked like an apple tree with apples all over the ground and three children picking them up. All done in bronze it was really beautiful.

"…oh! Clodagh…it's beautiful…they'll love it…" June ran her fingers through the golden fringe that trimmed the bottom of the shade she'd never seen such a lovely lamp.

They sat up for hours talking and laughing and crying and talking some more.

June left Clodagh in bed as she went off to work the next morning regretting not going to bed sooner the night before. But she'd be grand plenty of time for sleep when all the celebrations were over it was getting very close. She would call on Valerie after work to see how things were. Thinking to herself she hadn't heard from her in the last couple of days probably busy preparing for her big day. Joe answered the door looking at his face June knew straight away that something was up. Valerie pleasant as ever was sitting at her sewing machine at the kitchen table. When Joe left the room, all was revealed Joe had lost his job and he was devastated. It wasn't even so much the money end of things though it was very bad timing but Valerie had said how he had loved that job it wasn't an easy job and the pay wasn't great but the comradeship had made up for it.

He'd made some good friends working there the company had gone bust and they hadn't even got a week's notice. He worried that at his age no other company was going to offer him a job manual labour favoured the young. Valerie had sympathised with him but told him to try to put it aside until after the wedding and make the most of things they would survive they weren't alone or the worst off. There were men with young families that got the same news that day.

Joe had apologised for his situation and she had assured him that it wasn't of his doing and she wasn't going to hold it against him they'd had a little cry and she thought though she quietly worried about the bills coming in, that Joe was getting on with it. Obviously it wasn't the case he wore a look of defeat on his face though smiling through it his heart was broken. However the wedding was looming and there was no going back now job or no job!

As usual Valerie was organised down to the pins for the flowers. There were some things that were out of our control she'd said as she switched off her sewing machine.

She was well used to life throwing stuff at her down through the years she'd only be getting on top of things and some disaster or other would knock her down again such was life and you had to rise above it she'd added.

June admired her optimism but knew that she was so engrossed in the upcoming event that she hadn't given Joe's job a thought she felt it hadn't hit her yet it was tough but she did agree with her in one point she had made that life could be very unpredictable very unpredictable indeed.

Clodagh had done a bit of shopping while June was at work and had prepared a lovely roast dinner the smell met her as she walked up the garden path. It put her in mind of the days when Nan was around always a lovely meal ready to sit into of an evening.

"You shouldn't have…you were invited to stay for a rest not to be cooking dinner for me…" June lifted the lid on the pot of turnip and smiled it was her favourite vegetable and Clodagh knew it from the days they had worked together. There wasn't much they didn't know about each other back then. Dinner over they sat and chatted for a while June made a cup of tea she always liked a nice hot cup of tea after dinner wasn't much into deserts long as she had a nice cup of tea.

Clodagh spoke about her travels how the look in the children's eyes would haunt her forever.

June could see she was upset even in thinking about it. She went on to say that it took her a while to settle when she came home and she actually missed it still. June asked if any one thing had stuck out in her memory in working on the missions and she replied with a tear in her eye.

"Yes…that would be laughter…there was no laughter…innocent children caught up in a world of fighting and politics…there was no laughter June…I never saw them smile…or laugh."

Clodagh wiped the tear from her eye as June took her hand in hers.

Lying in bed June thought how she had been blessed with her childhood growing up in a loving home with enough to eat and although unknowingly missing out on a mother's love she was none the worst for it.

The post office was quiet the next day Agnes was already settled into her cup of tea when June got in, she jumped as Mr Oakley approached her desk and choked on her chocolate biscuit thumping her on the back June wasn't sure if he was enjoying it or if he was just panicking, he certainly put all he had into it anyway.

"Goodness…I could see stars there…whew! …good on you Mr O'…you shifted it fairly handy…went down the wrong way." Wiping the water from her eyes Agnes made her way to the toilet. On her return she commented in passing June's desk on how manly Mr O' was how strong though she reckoned she would be black and blue with all the thumping he was doing.

They were a thick as thieves again June was delighted, she didn't want any tension at the wedding and she did want them to go it was already a small crowd and she didn't want anyone opting out at this late stage.

Chapter 12

Valerie arrived at June's house with all her bits and pieces the wedding gown was hung carefully outside of the wardrobe and the shoes placed on the floor beneath it looked beautiful. She would wear her hair up. Greta was expected around later for a trial run very handy with the hairdressing she wouldn't hear of Valerie forking out good money when she could do it just as good and it would be her pleasure.

Not having met her before, June was excited to introduce Clodagh to Valerie. She had prepared some food and made some trifle as a treat a bit late to be worrying about the bulges in their outfits June decided a treat was in order.

Clodagh hadn't changed out of her nightwear and dressing gown having been chatting after breakfast and helping to prepare the food with June so she was upstairs getting changed when Valerie arrived.

"So nice to meet you at last." Valerie hugged her as she came into the kitchen.

They chatted like old friends and Clodagh remarked on the resemblance between Nan in the photograph on the mantle and Valerie. June agreed that her mother bore an unmistakable resemblance alright. Greta arrived full of the joys as usual and was delighted to see Clodagh again they talked right through

Valerie's hairdo. She made a lovely job of it too June was really impressed and it was decided that an up style was the way to go for the big day. Valerie looked very pleased with herself as she came from the bathroom after looking in the mirror. The three ladies awaiting her return complimented her as she walked back to the kitchen.

Greta looked a bit flushed but very proud of her work. With Clodagh staying Valerie would have to share a room with June though June offered to sleep on the sofa Valerie wouldn't hear of it. It wasn't as if there would be much sleep had that night they both agreed, June watched as her mother sat at the dressing table before going to bed and it put her in mind of her Nan. She would walk Greta home and be up to bed after.

She still remembered watching her Nan brush her long grey hair before tying it up in a bun at the back of her head she would put four clips each side of her head to keep it tidy and ask as she turned round to June who would be tumbling the wild cats on the bed behind her "Will I do?"

Walking Greta home, June's head was full of thoughts of Nan; she wasn't sure why and it had left her feeling very subdued. Greta noticing her being quiet asked if she was ok.

"Aw! …don't mind me Greta…I'm just tired…" She bid her goodnight and thanked her for the effort she had put into doing her mother's hair and for being the thoughtful friend she was to her.

Valerie having retired to the bedroom the house was quiet when she got back bar Clodagh standing at the sink washing the cups. There was no use in telling her to sit down and to enjoy being a guest in the house Clodagh by nature had to keep busy she had been the same in the post office always on the go.

Goodness, June thought to herself that seemed a lifetime ago now and Matt!

Well some days it seemed like a dream a nightmare and other days it was like it only happened yesterday but always a heartache that wouldn't go away.

"You'll never guess who I was talking to on my way here…bumped right into him in fact as I got off the train?" Clodagh had finished with the washing up and was now putting the kettle on and went on to rinse the teapot out to make a pot of tea. June would always rinse the teapot out after having tea but tonight there was too much going on. The teapot was left with the dried-up tea leaves in it, it was Nan's pet hate she always said it would stain the inside of the pot and the tea wouldn't taste the same. She too loved her cup of tea but it had to be in a cup mind never a big mug and a china cup at that!

"Who?" June sat at the table feeling like the day had taken its toll. She was ready for bed.

"…Mac! …remember Mac! …Malcolm Mac Phearson…your old boss?"

Clodagh began to laugh.

"…aw Mac…ya…how is he? …what brings him back to town…thought he'd gone for good."

Clodagh carrying the two cups of tea to the table looked sort of mischievous, June thought to herself. Seems she'd only spoken to him briefly but he had apologized for being in a rush and insisted they would meet later in the week before she returned to stay with her aunt Daisy. He'd enquired about June and asked Clodagh to give her his best regards.

"...what do you think...maybe come with me...for old time's sake!" There definitely was a look of mischief in her eyes.

Valerie was packing her bits into her bag when June came into the bedroom bidding Clodagh goodnight on the landing.

No sleep on her mother tonight, she'd thought and all she wanted to do was collapse on the bed but she would have to pluck up some energy from somewhere. This was a very special night a night she would never have dreamed of having a couple of years back never have dreamed of meeting her mother let alone have her stay in her house in her bedroom.

They chatted for hours awaking at first light June realised she had slept in her clothes must have conked while talking to her mother.

Turning over to the other side of the bed she realised that her mother was already up and out of the bed she wondered if Clodagh was up as well.

Yawning she walked down the stairs she always walked sideways on the stairs they were very narrow steps and Nan always walked that way so she did too.

There was a lovely smell coming from the kitchen Clodagh was making pancakes and there was no sign of Valerie. Without having to ask her whereabouts Clodagh told her she had gone to the cemetery to visit her mam and dad. That didn't really surprise June it was like something she herself would have done.

If ever there was an occasion a birthday or anniversary her own birthday even June would always go to visit them to make them a part of the day. She reckoned Valerie was doing the same making them a part of her special day.

Starving she ate far too many pancakes leaving her bloated and full to the brim.

They were delicious while eating them but it was like they swell up inside and it felt like you'd eaten ten times as many. Getting the range set to light she decided she would have her bath early and leave time for Clodagh and Valerie to have the bathroom to themselves to get ready. There would be loads of water if she kept the fire going.

She thought about Mac and the good times they'd had while working together in the post office which seemed like a lifetime ago now. She wondered what he might make of Mr O' and Agnes. Now! There was a character!

"Bathroom is free." She shouted at the top of her voice from the landing and scattered into the bedroom her towel only covered so much and she didn't want to shock anyone. She was feeling more excited today the day before she just felt exhausted. She would wear her tracksuit for the time being much too early to get dressed up and she wanted to keep an eye on the fire to make sure there was enough hot water for everyone.

"Sit down…I have something to show you." Valerie pulled the chair from beneath the table and ushered her to sit on it. Hair dripping wet June had decided to let it dry naturally for a while it lessened the frizz a bit and she would roll it when was almost dry. The kitchen was like a sauna Clodagh had put the coal on the fire and left the dampers open the flame was raging up the chimney. She would see to it as soon as she had seen whatever it was her mother wanted to show her, she seemed so excited about it.

"I went to the cemetery first thing…" Valerie took her coat from the hall and all thumbs proceeded to root in both pockets all a fluster she came to the table holding both hands out in front of June.

"…it's a feather June…I was just standing there not even thinking…just looking at their names on the headstone…and it sort of floated…right in front of my face." A tear in her eye she continued "…it's a sign…it's a sign of an angel."

June took the delicate white feather in her hand her mother wiped her tear-stained face "…I cried all the way back…it was…such a wonderful feeling June…like…like they were wishing me happiness on my wedding day."

What a lovely start to the day, June thought as she watched her mother carefully place the feather on the mantelpiece behind the old photograph of her mother and father Nan and Pop. Placing a kiss on each face she smiled.

"Are you happy?" June took her hand as she walked by to go upstairs to have her bath.

"…I have never been so happy." She kissed June on the head and went upstairs.

Greta arrived to do her hairdressing bit and as usual lift the spirits there was banter and laughter tears and memories all rolled into a couple of hours that they would all remember for the rest of their days.

Then there was panic Joe's friend and best man Vincent had got up to find his car wouldn't start he was the bride's chauffer to the church due at the house to pick her up within the hour. June had answered the phone and wanted to keep the news from Valerie for fear of panic. She would have to think of something signalling quietly to Greta she spoke to her in the hall out of earshot of Valerie and Clodagh who were busy deciding which colour nail varnish Valerie should wear.

Greta was worried this was indeed a bit bothersome!

Deep in thought they both jumped as the doorbell rang. Agnes stood in her finery looking like a lady of the manner.

"I have been to four different houses looking for you…I knew you lived around here but wasn't sure where…finally I found someone at home…and they sent me here…must be all in bed." She continued to talk as she proceeded down the hallway.

"…hope it was ok to call." Turning back to where June and Greta were standing.

She had wondered if maybe she could offer anybody a lift to the church.

Mr O' was just closing up shop at the post office as she spoke and there was room for two or even three in the back of the car.

"…the thought just entered my head as I got into the car…he wouldn't mind at all…plenty of room."

June looked at Greta and smiled filling Agnes in on their predicament she told her she had been sent by an angel to save the day. Valerie would be travelling in style to the church Mr O' had a beautiful car sparkling as always it glistened in the sun. The day had been kind to her as well with sunshine all the way.

Looking a bit puzzled Valerie got into the car with Mr O' done up to the last and ever the gentleman holding the door open for her. *He almost seemed cheerful which was most unusual for him*, June thought to herself but she wouldn't knock it not today. Today he was her knight in shining armour.

Valerie looked back as she carefully sat into the car June smiled and assured her all would be revealed later.

Arrangements had been made to pick up Vincent and Gabi with the ring boy Teddy they'd decided baby Blossom would be best staying with her grandma.

It was a beautiful service June had felt both happy and sad. What a joy it would have been to have her Nan and Pop there and Matt dear Matt forever engrained in her memory a love that was never to be!

The day went off without a hitch very simple absolutely no extravagance just a small gathering of close friends and family. June being the only family member to speak of with Joe not having any family of his own.

Not so now they looked like the happiest couple June had ever seen they had nothing of value in their belongings but had something money couldn't buy.

"Morning...thought I wouldn't see you for a few hours yet!"

June was surprised to see Clodagh drinking tea at the kitchen table as she came down the stairs.

"Wasn't it a great day? ...from start to finish...I don't think I was ever made to feel as welcome...they're lovely people...aren't they?"

They chatted for hours Clodagh would be catching the first train the next day she'd promised her aunt she would be back and she knew she would be beginning to fret by now. She'd lived alone for years but of late she had become a bit dependant on Clodagh but she didn't mind. She too was glad of the company.

She'd asked June if she would accompany her into the village in the afternoon to meet Mac, June hesitated but Clodagh insisted that he would be so glad to see her again and he had asked for her. Her brief meeting with him at the train station was such a joy to her she knew June would love to see him again too.

Browsing through her very much in need of updating wardrobe June wasn't really in the mood but when would she see Clodagh again after this? goodness knows. Her head felt sort of fuzzy not that she'd been drinking too much the day before she'd thought but it was probably the stress of the lead up to the wedding.

Valerie and Joe would be calling round for tea so it would have to be a short visit into the village she could manage that!

As they approached the same old coffee shop where June had met her mother for the first time she started to think back, so much had happened in that short time. Seeing Mac wave from the window was like meeting an old friend again though time had lapsed it was like they'd chatted yesterday he'd been in town on business and was heading back to the city on the next train.

"Lovely to meet up again." He kissed June on the cheek as they parted leaving her in a state of blushing, she didn't know why after all it was just Mac!

She would do a nice bit of roast for the tea for the newlyweds and of course it was going to be the last meal she would share with Clodagh too for God knows how long. She would make an extra effort make some trifle for desert just like Nan used to make. Valerie would like that. Turned out Joe was the big trifle fan June didn't know where he had put it all he'd scraped his plate after the dinner and had asked for a second helping of trifle.

The conversation of course went on all night taking in the wedding ceremony the guests the fun and also the sadness attached to the day.

Clodagh was the first to leave the table followed by Valerie and Joe June watched as Joe took Valerie's hand as they walked down the hall to the door a cab awaited them at the gate feeling a sudden loneliness June gasped as she waved her mother and Joe off at the door.

"Be happy you two." She whispered as they went out of sight.

As she opened the door to the post office next day wanting to be anywhere else but there June had it in her head to thank Agnes for organising a lift for her mother to the church at the very last minute and indeed Mr O' for obliging willingly.

Though thinking about it she'd thought to herself, *he probably didn't have a choice in the matter Agnes could be very persuasive!*

Agnes spent the morning rubbing her bunion while Mr O' was nowhere to be seen.

"We had a lovely time Jane…really lovely…sure I had a couple too many roast potatoes…if you know what I mean." Agnes with a look of devilment in her eyes winked mischievously at June.

Turned out Mr O' wasn't too impressed either.

"…sure it isn't often we get to let our hair down is it?" Agnes got up to go to the toilet complaining of having aches and pains where she never had aches and pains before she was like a tonic.

Dizzy with thoughts June strolled home.

As she came up the garden path the phone was ringing in the hall.

Hoping not to miss the call she ran to the door it was Clodagh she thanked her for lovely few days and looked forward to seeing her again soon.

June had hoped it would be Valerie calling although it was so nice to hear from Clodagh too. The house was eerily quiet it was the first time she'd been on her own for a while and she was missing the company.

Greta had been watching for her to pass the gate and was disappointed when she hadn't called in it was a lovely evening and she'd baked an apple tart so she decided to call by and say hello she knew June would have a quiet house and would probably be missing the activity. June was so delighted to see her she'd decided not to call into Greta that evening because she had been kept so busy in the few days before the wedding and indeed on the day that she thought she would give her a bit of space to relax. Greta could tell June was feeling a bit down it was only natural after all the excitement she was probably a bit tired too she'd thought.

"What about you giving us a day out?" Greta was helping herself to the leftover cream in the fridge "…can't have apple pie without a dollop of cream."

June shrugged her shoulders.

"Me? Greta there would be more chance of finding a frog in your ear."

They both laughed.

"…aw! …you never know…you know what they say now June…every pot has a lid…just have to find it."

Some chance, June thought to herself and she thought of Matt!

As she opened the door of the post office next morning Mr O' approached her from behind her desk she wondered what had brought him there he'd never come over to ask her anything or say anything he would always stand at the counter.

Was there something wrong with her work?

"Ahem..." He cleared his throat and continued, "Don't like my staff taking personal calls during working hours...I've taken a message but only this once mind." He brushed past her at an awful speed pointing to the piece of paper he'd left on her desk. June thanked him and apologised wondering what he was talking about she'd never in all her years working there received a personal call.

The note was very brief "Ring me, Mac..." with a phone number written underneath. June took the piece of paper and put it in her bag she certainly wouldn't be ringing him from work maybe later or maybe not. Why would he want her to ring him anyway?

Agnes came through the door like a hurricane.

"How's the form today with you know who? ...want to take an extra hour at lunchtime...there's a sale on in town that I want to go to...saw a lovely scarf on the window..." June smiled at her and thought to herself.

"Good luck with that..." He was in a ferocious mood could hear him giving out from his office but she thought to herself, *Agnes will get around him.*

Having made three attempts to ask him Agnes had all but given up on wandering into the sale when Mr O' announced he had a meeting and would be gone for the rest of the day.

You could light a cigarette with the smile on Agnes's face he wasn't outside the door when she had her coat on.

"...wish me luck." And she was gone within minutes.

June had to laugh she wished she herself could be more carefree.

Weighed down with bags Agnes appeared about three hours later very pleased with her purchases and nothing would do her only to go through each item with June the original price and the sale price. There would be no more work done for the rest of the afternoon. Agnes fitted on every item and paraded it in front of June for her approval.

Chapter 13

"Where's the scarf? …I thought you went in especially for the scarf?"

Seemed the scarf had sold within minutes of opening time she'd been disappointed so decided to treat herself to a few bits to cheer herself up.

She was something else June thought, *they'd definitely broken the mould!*

Passing Greta's house June thought she would drop in for a chat she'd done a shepherd's pie the day before so she would heat it up again for dinner the evening was her own with no cooking to do. Although there were plenty of other chores she could be doing but all she wanted was to put her feet up with a nice cup of tea. She was surprised to see Valerie answer the door.

"I was a bit early so I said I'd call to Greta for an hour…catch up on all the gossip."

They both laughed and hugged each other.

"So…how's married life treating you?"

Looking at her mother June could see her eyes still glowed as she spoke about Joe what a wonderful thing this must be she'd thought and wondered if she'd held that glow when she was with Matt. The eyes are the windows to the soul her Nan would say she certainly loved Matt with all of her heart and all her soul.

Maybe to others she'd glowed with happiness that love that she had shared with Matt, the loss of which had almost consumed her had almost left her broken.

Greta was out of the kitchen carrying a tray of homemade scones tea and jam and cream June sighed as she sat back and enjoyed every crumb.

Holding the phone in one hand and the piece of paper where Mr O' had taken down the number in the other she wondered again why Mac would be ringing her.

Turned out he was thinking of extending his business in the city and would be looking for extra staff he'd wondered if maybe his best staff member from the post office might be interested. They laughed she was his only staff member she reminded him.

"Think about it June…there's no rush…won't be for a couple of months yet…say you'll at least give it some thought?" She'd agreed to give it some thought if only to please him but moving to the city? She'd never had any thoughts of moving to the city and she didn't think she ever would she didn't go into the city much but on any occasion that she did she couldn't wait to get out of there and back to the fresh sea air and the quiet.

The offer of extra money was indeed tempting and Mac would organise accommodation nearby for her and there was the getting away from Mr O'.

She would think about it as she said she would but she knew in her heart that the answer would be the same.

Mac was disappointed but understood she'd thanked him for the offer and wished him well in his new venture.

She had never remembered Joe calling by without Valerie so when she opened the front door for a moment her heart had sank.

Inviting him in she went straight to the kitchen to put the kettle on.

He was quiet she'd thought she'd felt he was making small talk.

She didn't want to seem rude in asking where Valerie was so she waited for him to mention her he was on his second cup of tea when he'd told her there was something he had to tell her. She was frightened now she'd felt a chill going down her spine it was bad news she knew it was.

Joe had come home to find Valerie lying on the couch out of it with a drink.

June gasped, "Why? …she was so happy…why would she?"

It hadn't been the first time he'd come home to find her drinking but this time she was out of it. He'd wondered if June might have a word with her.

But how could she approach this when she hadn't had a clue as to what was going on as far as she could see everything was rosy, she seemed so happy and settled into married life.

She would call round unannounced the next day after work.

As she walked up the path, she almost changed her mind her thoughts of her mother had been such happy ones of late and she didn't want that taken away from her she didn't want to see her mother in any other light other than the happy smiling face she now knew.

"Hi…come on in…"

Valerie seemed just fine her usual cheery self as she opened the door.

Or was she almost too cheery?

Watching her potter around her tiny little kitchen June wasn't sure and she hated herself for thinking that way the room was nice and tidy fresh flowers on the middle of the table very homely.

"Mam…" June stopped for a moment she wanted to come clean with her and tell her that Joe had come round and was worried about her but would she ruin everything. The lovely relationship they had built up over the last couple of years despite everything.

"…just a minute June…I need the bathroom…was just heading there when the doorbell rang…won't be a tick…"

Sitting at the table June was tempted to check the cupboards to see if there was any drink stashed away looking at her mother fixing her hair in the mirror in the hall put her in mind of her Nan, she had so many of her traits.

"…sorry love what were you saying?" June asked her where she had got the beautiful flowers. This was harder than she thought.

"…come and sit on the sofa…nice to relax with a cup of tea…"

Valerie left the tea and biscuits on the coffee table in front of the sofa fluffing up the cushions before June sat down. As she lifted one of the cushions a small glass vodka bottle fell on the floor. Quickly picking it up she put it in a bin under the sink making a clashing noise which told June there was more than one bottle there. A tear came into June's eye as she watched her mother carry on as normal.

She didn't know a lot about alcoholism but she did hear that the victim would hide it well.

June had her tea and ate a biscuit with a lump in her throat she couldn't bring herself to address this today not now she would mull over it for a few days see how best to approach it without offending her.

Greta was shocked when June decided to call on her on the way home and ask her advice. Greta knew how much the relationship meant to both June and indeed her mother they would have to be very cautious.

Agnes had noticed June being very quiet the next day at work not wanting to pry she had offered her a sympathetic ear June assured her that everything was fine and that she was just feeling a bit under the weather.

She thought of Matt and the problems the curse of drink had brought to his family if only he were here she'd thought, *if only she'd had someone to talk to, confide in.*

Joe had taken ill at work and the foreman had been knocking on Valerie's door to let her know and when she hadn't answered he'd put a slip of paper in the letterbox. Valerie had overslept and was in a right tizzy when she turned up on June's door.

"He never works Saturdays…they were busy so he obliged…in fact he seems to be working all the hours God sends these days…June I'm so worried." Valerie went on to say Joe was bending over backwards to please his new employer.

June made her a cup of tea and went to answer the door it was Greta she'd been to the market and spotted Valerie walking a bit ahead of her down the road. She'd shouted but